Romeo Returns

Leon J. Gratton

Grosvenor House
Publishing Limited

All rights reserved
Copyright © Leon J. Gratton, 2024

The right of Leon J. Gratton to be identified as the author of this
work has been asserted in accordance with Section 78
of the Copyright, Designs and Patents Act 1988

The book cover is copyright to Leon J. Gratton

This book is published by
Grosvenor House Publishing Ltd
Link House
140 The Broadway, Tolworth, Surrey, KT6 7HT.
www.grosvenorhousepublishing.co.uk

This book is sold subject to the conditions that it shall not, by way of
trade or otherwise, be lent, resold, hired out or otherwise circulated
without the author's or publisher's prior consent in any form of
binding or cover other than that in which it is published and
without a similar condition including this condition being
imposed on the subsequent purchaser.

This book is a work of fiction. Any resemblance to
people or events, past or present, is purely coincidental.

A CIP record for this book
is available from the British Library

ISBN 978-1-80381-936-5

Chapter 1

There is a world, a world between worlds, a world of shadows and light, where martial arts is dominant and Ninja rule. This is where they come to do their shadow trials. Where Demon Tengu and Holy Samurai face each other. The Nine Halls of Death and Jin Go world of spiritual attainment. This is where Romeo Greene's body has come to seek final judgement, to be bathed in martial fire of action and energy of the Jin Go, many secret's lie awaiting The death of masters. The Nin Po world, undiluted and taken to the degrees of skill. Master versus master, trial after trial, blood, bone and energy, and muscle and spirit. The Tengu Demons, the Jian warrior cult, the dragons watch closely on the different styles of each master. They will end up being attuned to a dragon. Who have such powers as to bring back the dead. Smile into the eyes of the great golden serpent. One of them at least.

Wake Up

Wake Up

Chapter 2

Giros smiled as he finished tying his Gi with a crimson sash. He was told he may have to go on a pilgrimage. A holy journey into the mountains of China, in search of the Wu Dang Mountain. Where he had to find a rare Temple of Knowledge. A rare energy point of true wisdom and great compassion. He looked into the night, breathing slowly and circulating his Chi. He smiled as he saw into the spirit world. He witnessed the joining of Romeo and Julie. He also watched as the blood was washed off his Dragon Tattoo. He was to go and make his sojourn, his mystical pilgrimage.

Kikieo sat in a lotus next to him. She was willing to go into that realm of spirituality. A tear ran down her cheek at the thought of having to retrieve her saviour and lover, bring him back from the dead in this world, it would only be for a couple of months. But in that time she would fill with courage and spirit, she would truly be Shinobi, all her doubts and fears would transcend into the Jin Go world. She would traverse the plane of earthly realm into the mysterious shadow world of Ninjutsu, it wouldn't be easy as she had to go under cloak and veil. No one would recognise her except Romeo whom she had to save and bring him back to his own world. Giros and herself had their hands full and Jason Kendricks was to watch over them as they travelled into the Jin Go world. He could have no part to play in the shadowy realm where all martial artists were destined to go. First things first, they would have to travel deep into Asia and into Indochina where they would have to get blessed and trained by the Shaolin Monks where they would also get the supreme Monk's blessing before they had to do their Twelve-day meditation with no food or water for the first five days. Then light rice dinners, as they had to become more dead than alive. And this was a vital part of their journey. They would become more in tune with the realm of death, it was in all ways not an easy way to traverse. No they would come across extreme pain psychic pain that was hidden from most martial artists. And only the most astute and hardened had made it from Earth to the shadowy death like world, Jin Go.

They would be completely at the will of the Dragon. They would have to strike without putting energy into it they were going to find Romeos spirit as instructed by the old Shidoshi. There were two reasons for this, one was to insure the passing of the Shidoshi into the next world and the second to make sure Kikieo was satisfied with Romeo's rest. Giro's smiled at his sister cousin, and made sure his Gi was on correctly. Kikieo smiled back and began to murmur the incantations and make the mystical symbols of Ninja Kanji.

Then she started to make the Kuji hand shapes that contained the knowledge that she had learned. She finished each shapes with the Zen shape, then she relaxed with the back of her hands resting on her thighs. As she did this she breathed out sharply. Then continued to say the slow chant for each of her skills.

"Toi, Shu, Retsu, Zen." And the rest. She focused her Ki into her Hari and began to circulate the energies in the meridians down her left hand side. She then concentrated all her mystic energy and began to travel spiritually into the world of Jin Go. Giros did the same but his pattern was slightly different to Kikieo's. He had learned a slightly different approach than Kikieo. He had travelled to the dragon realm before and knew how treacherous and dangerous it was. He smiled as he bowed to the small shape of the Mata Hari as she came closer, "Hide your fear," He said, "As it leaves a distinct trail." He continued then finished, "An astral ripple of energy in the colour of Yellow".

She smiled, did the sign of sword finger and concentrated on covering her fear. This seemed to help speed her energy and the more she concentrated the more it came with ease. She was ready to walk the shadow dragon realm. Then she grew more and more in confidence, the further into the realm she traversed. She had chi and fluidity that was gathering more in strength and helping her calm the confusing realm that she was in. Giros knew what he was doing, he had been a Shinobi for as long as he could remember and found the movement in that world as easy as anything that he had done in a number of ways. No he was practiced and attuned to the dragon realm. He made the traversing of the Earth realm to the Astral realm to the Dragon realm seem easy.

Kikieo bowed back and they headed towards the scared chamber of Dragons and death. The whole kingdom of Dragons and the nine sacred halls of Death. That was supposed to be the last place you go to train before you die. And was therefore almost synonymous with the death of a true Martial artist. Some took the

Jade palace some the dragons golden room. Others it was the tiger chi of thought. It was very personal and there were many different ways. Some came stealthily, some ready and equipped for action. Others it was a place of healing. And others a place of serenity. Many poet, Artist and warrior had been down this path but few who came unprepared were successful. It was forbidden and only the masters of the Dark arts were considered worthy of the Journey. Many a ninja and Karateka had realised to their demise that only the most studious and athletic were worthy of its secrets so it was the logical place to find Romeo. Kikeo smiled and began to listen with her Inner ear. She knew that in all likely hood Romeo would be in the Golden palace of the dragon getting healing and joining his lady, Julie. She thought she could hear the whispers of Romeo and his Lover Julie. She listened more intently. And wandered onto the Path of the Golden dragon. Giros followed suite. She could hear him laughing and gently kissing his lover. 'Boy is he going to love me interrupting his reunion' She thought as she set upon the path of the Golden dragon. Giros smiled as he could also hear the loving reunion of Romeo. It took six days walk in the shadowy world and all around they could feel ninja and various other schools of Martial Arts surrounding them. They had to be careful as at any moment they could be tested with their martial prowess. But for some strange reason they were getting the golden treatment and the shadowy dimension that it was, was giving them a pass. Giros was very cautious as he had been here a couple of times and every time it had got bloody. And brutal.

Chapter 3

Romeo was smiling as he kissed and caressed his lover. They were laughing and having no cause for concern, no they were blessed with the reunion of the two of them. The Golden Dragon's guardians who had heard of Romeo's plight with both the Hell's Angels and the Lin Qua. Had opened their arms and let the two lovers enter their confines and use their foods and healing herbs. All they asked in return was the pair of them pray to its deity, The Golden Dragon of Wisdom. Which had last been seen before Christ and before Buddha. The Golden Dragon of Wisdom had been around since before time was prevalent. Giros got into the fourth day of travel and smiled. Many an accomplished martial artist had gone mad long before now. Especially when they had never seized an invitation into the Golden Dragon's den. But that was the sacrifice they had foolishly made before entering the Jin Go world. They had basically forgot the etiquette and had neither the brains nor the skills to use in the Jin Go world. In other words they had ended out of their depth and out of their mind.

Romeo smiled as he began to make love to his lady and as he had done countless times. She was receptive to his touch, his breath, his muscular body. No, this was heaven to her and him. She watched him when he first arrived to bathe his hands and body and cleanse himself of all the blood that had been attached to him during his journey, into revenge. And he was steady and fast as he was shown to Julies room. He drank the Holy Juice of the Jade and was offered beautiful ripe fruit and berries. This was done ceremoniously so and three times a day. He was also offered the meat of bird and cattle, he smiled as the Shaolin who guarded the sacred dragons keep. Kept them safe, as if they had made the worlds both of the Jin Go and Earth (as well as the rest) safer. Then the gates to the keep were thumped and Giros and Kikieo stood there with hands in Buddha, showing that they were harmless to the people of the Dragon of Wisdom.

The gates opened and both the Mati Hari and Shinobi walked through. Romeo stood and watched as the pair of Koga were approached by the Shaolin and other Monks of orders like the Lotus Palm and Masters of Flowers. There was no harm or malice as the Two walked slowly to the Temple's Halls where the monks were studious and learning. The ancient teachers taught their student and taught them well, some hand-to-hand, others weapons and some healing arts. The further in to the halls of wisdom they were trained in subterfuge and deception and certain skills, like laying traps, and picking locks and also magic, time stop and various other spells like invisibility and blink travel. These were all sacred things that had vanished out the world centuries ago. Suddenly there's magic. Romeo had got lost in the writings of various Buddhas and Bramahs monks and nuns, or as they are known Onis. He had a very good knowledge when he went in to the Golden Dragon of Wisdoms keep. But now several years later he was full to the brim with knowledge. Two Shaolin dressed in leopard skins round their wrists and orange robes. They smiled at the two Ninja. And said in ancient Mandarin.

"You come as guests and will be treated thus."

They then showed the two of them to rooms Bamboo mats and paper walls and doors each room had its own wooden tub. They both bowed to the Monks and went and dressed in the local garb. They then followed the rest of the guests including Romeo and Julie. They sat around and ate rice balls and various Peeking dishes. Giro's and Kikieo finished their meal then went over to Romeo and his lady. Romeo stood up and bowed to the Ninja's. He then smiled and introduced Julie to Kikieo and Giros. The Ninja had only a few short days to convince Romeo to come back to the Earth realm and help the old Shidoshi in his dark times that he had to endure. He was getting weaker by the day and was focusing his energies and aligning his spirit to the fact that he was dying. But something was wrong, something had upset the old Grandmaster and was shadowing his very spirit. It was some kind of old ancient Shinobi Demon, and it was hungry and waiting for the Old Grandmaster to pass into the Jin Go realm. Where it would devour the old man's spirit and leave him lost with no hope of reincarnation. He would be left to wander the outer rim of the Jin Go realm. No hope of meeting his family and no hope of ever being a human again, he would be a wandering ghost with a very dim light for a centre. He was troubled deeply by this, his greatest achievement could not help him in this situation. He needed Romeo, and the other two to battle with this demon. And all the Ninja forces it had unleashed onto the Earth realm. This was dangerous and deadly task he would have to undertake. Romeo read the scroll that Kikieo had been given before travelling to the Jin Go realm. Romeo sighed as he finished the scroll, completing it with a Ketsu flick of his hand and rolled the scroll up. He smiled solemnly and stayed quiet for a few minutes deeply contemplating the task that he would surely undertake. He smiled after thinking what his options were. He knew little about Shinobi Demons. Only that they were fierce savage creatures that seldom lost a battle. This one in particular was known for its possession of Shinobi's spirits and using their bodies to full effect. It had many ways to do this, breathing in the essence then taking control of the Ninjas spirit. This was then used to trick the party of Ninjas and if possible kill the rest of the Ninjas. This particular demon had done this many times and had satiated its Devil Master with fresh dead spirit. That the Devil would feast on the dead spirit then grow more in strength, tipping the balance of the holy and unholy. The scroll said that they didn't have a lot of time but Romeo had completed most of the Golden Dragons spirit tests and had picked up a few new tricks. He had learned a few spells and new hand to hand techniques. He was also now an adept in healing. Something he was studying whilst he was alive. But only the Golden Dragon Monks knew the latter half of his training and that would be vital to his survival and also the other two Ninja. He smiled, as it was coming back to him more and more every day in the beautiful mystical Golden Dragons keep. He had been greeted at the Gates by Julie and a number of different monks. They instantly took a shine to Romeo and Romeo did to them. He was with his Lady and that was the best part about it. He would never go without, he had all the knowledge of the Golden Dragons spirit to content himself with.

He sighed and looked at Giros and Kikeo, "We leave the day after tomorrow".

It was a short stay but the Mata Hari and the Shinobi were glad to get a look around the keep. They spent the remainder of their time reading dragon scrolls and watching the arts be used in both defence and offense. The hour before they left they were gifted with mystical lock picks and enough herbs to help them out in times of trouble. They began to make their journey to the Astral gate where they would be sent back to the Earth realms. They sat the three of them all in half lotus and began to shape shift through the basic skills that they had acquired over many years of martial arts and the study of Ninjutsu. They began to shift through the dimension that they were in and as night turned to day they returned to Earth. Jason was stood over the three of them as their life came back into their bodies. Giros, Kikeo and Romeo all gasped for breath as the sulphuric atmosphere was fired out of their bodies.

Jason smiled and said, "Alright Shidoshi alright friends".

He then handed each of them a cup of Japanese green tea to wet their dead and deathly lungs. The four of them left the house and went out to get breakfast. They went to a small café just on the outskirts of Little Tokyo and they ate in a rather greedy fashion the all American breakfast, that included pancakes, bacon and eggs (any way they wanted them). After the food and coffee was consumed, they began to discuss what their options were. They had a tricky situation to deal with no they were in a bit of a mess knowing that this Demon (Tengu) was holding all the cards. And they had very little of scope to deal with the Demon. No they had to be sure when and what to hit as the Demon would come at them as friends, pupils or local martial artists.

Chapter 4

The Old Shidoshi was lying on the floor of his room waiting for word from his niece and most venerable student Giros. He smiled and rested his eyes for a few more minutes. Then the weather changed into the frozen cold winter weather that wasn't due for another two three months. It hit and woke his pleasant slumber. He walked through to the training room and picked up a Bokken one that happened to be Shuzi's favourite. He smiled as he weighed the thing in his hand. He was an expert Iado swordsman so knew exactly where the weight and how short his grip would have to be. But no one had even come close to winning a challenge with him as he was so fast it was like lightning striking, especially when he had been challenged with Katana.

For ninety years he had been on this, for seventy of them he had trained in Katana. He was an adept at Iado. And well the rest of the Ninjitsu system was well, easy. He had made his reputation undefeated and now in his ninetieth year he still was lightning fast. The Old Shidoshi was ready for the Tengu Demon and his master. He knew it was a major Arcane Devil that was pulling the strings of the Tengu. He began to wonder if he had what it took to challenge such a creature of vast darkness and supernatural powers. Then the phone rang. He put the Bokken back onto the rack and answered the Phone.

"Ah Mr Greene, just in time, how was your visit into the Jin Go world?"

Romeo smiled and replied, "It couldn't have been any better".

The Koga Shidoshi smiled and replied, "As long as you are up to this next arduous task?" He asked with a little hint of sarcasm.

Romeo smiled at the Jibe and asked, "When do you suppose the Tengu will strike?"

The old Shidoshi smiled, "If am not mistaken, the demon will hit you four with everything it's got".

"Leaving me vulnerable and at its mercy." Romeo smiled, "It's never as simple as a straight up fight".

The Shidoshi smiled again and said, "No nothing is clear cut when it comes to a Tengu".

Romeo sighed slightly knowing that the old Shidoshi was spot on the money. "Where are we best situated to fight this creature?"

The Shidoshi sighed and said, "In a temple or in a church. But that is easier said than done". He continued. Romeo carried on the conversation for fifteen minutes or so. He told the old Shidoshi all about the Golden Dragon keep and it's secrets. He made healthy references to his lover. And various lessons that he had learned whilst still remaining focused.

Chapter 5

The Tengu lifted his frame up off the floor. Stretching his body and almost touching the ceiling. That was a good twelve feet from the floor. He snarled and showed his elongated canine teeth. He was beginning to formulate a plan, a plan that would eradicate the four Ninja, he was in the spirit of the Shinobi. And knew his skills at martial arts were more than enough to face the four of them. His skin glistened red and his muscles were throbbing with veins and also shaped as a muscle bound athlete. He was quite the specimen, he began to practice the demon Kata. That very few had seen and fewer had survived its use. He was an adept, a genius, as one would say. He had never lost a fight, and thus made one of the deadliest of adversaries. He was also not alone as a full hand and foot were preparing themselves to fight Romeo and his enclave of Koga Ninja. This he thought was not going to be easy. In fact the ways that Romeo had learned whilst in the Jin Go world made him more deadly, and faster with spells that he had learned whilst in that world. But the Tengu still remained confident and thought little of the Ninja Romeo, he was certain that they were no match for him.

He then knelt after finishing his Kata. And began to shape shift through his consciousness and into one of the Nine Planes of Hell. He would meet hopefully with his Devil Master; Seth, lord of decay. Then he would get the ancient demon scroll with its various rites of power and magic. He knew that this would be a game changer and would only be needed if all else failed. He snarled as he was approached by two bone Demons, who were charged with the task of guarding the Devil Seth.

"Let him through," Boomed the voice of Seth. The two guards split leaving him free to go to his Master. The Tengu knew he was safe knowing he was doing all that was expected of him in the task of eradicating the last of the Koga. With the Old man being the last to die.

Seth smiled and said, "Ah Master Tengu you are carrying out my instructions?"

The Tengu let a small, murmured growl escape. This was a sign of compliance and doing his lords business. Seth carried on, "You know the task is more difficult than you imagine?"

The Tengu curled his lip and replied, "Yes Master".

Seth smiled and took a bite of his human feast of organs and limbs. "Good," He said and drank a dark as pitch goblet of blood.

The Tengu got down on one knee. "Anything for you Master," He said.

Then the Tengu stood up and headed back out of the room that was made of bone and blood. "Oh and demon, you fail I will roast you for supper"

The Tengu growled in his throat and left the Plane of Hell and went back to earth.

Chapter 6

Romeo began to make a bed to sleep in, and Kikieo asked quietly, "Can I join you in sleep?"

Romeo smiled at the young Mati Hari, "I am back rejoined with my lady. Do not take offence, I have rekindled the love that was ever my quest".

Kikieo smiled and looked at Romeo, "I understand".

Romeo smiled and replied, "Please try".

Giros and Jason were through in the sitting room discussing how difficult the Tengu was to kill. Jason had only a limited knowledge of Japanese Demons. And one thing he knew for sure was that they were almost impossible to kill. That certain spells and magic was part of their make-up and they knew how to use the dead, bring them back and that made the ones that were dead become nigh on impossible to kill. Not like zombies, but more like the immortal doaists of ancient China and Japan. It was these things and how adept in fighting the Tengu was that made this task arduous and very near impossible.

Jason smiled. "This was turning out to be interesting," He said, then sipped some of his green tea from Japan.

Giros smiled and looked out into the distance. He then rolled out his Futon and said, "Take it easy, Jason we are not helpless in this fight".

Jason nodded his head and rolled out his futon next to him. The two of them fell into a vast peaceful sleep. Kikieo joined them after a small cry to herself in the hall. Romeo noticed as she sobbed. He mentally kicked himself. Knowing only the love that he held for each of them.

Julie was watching over him in the Golden Dragons seeing room. And she was saddened by the display, she smiled and said quietly to Romeo, "Take her my lover you know you have enough love to share".

Romeo sat up and said, "Kikieo come back".

Kikieo stopped sobbing and returned to the room, she lay in his arms and they both drifted off into a calm relaxed sleep. Romeo smiled as if heaven had blessed him in all ways and forms. The old Shidoshi also smiled in the dim lit room of shadows where he was praying for heavenly help. 'Ahh' he thought 'A big heart he has'. 'And the wisdom of a grand master' he continued.

"May dragons of golden wisdom see you safe in this fight". Said the old Shidoshi.

Chapter 7

The Tengu Demon, Lustrain, smiled as it dined on the corpse of a dead black belt whom he had duped into his clutches. Lustrain then attacked the young twenty-year-old black belt and began to devour him cold and heartily. He had seduced the young black belt with promise of a beautiful young girl, showing all kinds of leg and breast. This had really worked as the young martial artist had followed the illusion into Lustrain the demons lair. Where the Tengu had struck and struck hard from the shadows. The young Karateka never knew what had hit him. The martial artist tried to roll and front kick the massive Demon who took the powerful Mi Geri (front kick) and didn't even flinch. He then Grappled trying to use his body weight and Hip strength to his advantage, but this did no good as the Demon was sure footed and stood fast and steady. Lustrain began to laugh as he choked the life out of the Karateka. The young martial artist was no use against the powerful demon. He finished the young man then began to cook him over a large fire pit. Him and several Ninja's dined fresh on the corpse of the young man. They disposed of the bones of the karateka in a pile that had been gathering up over the past year or so.

"Thank you Gentlemen, that will be all for just now," Boomed Lustrain. The Ninja decided to leave the

Tengu to his thoughts and meditations. They slipped carefully back into the shadows. Knowing only that they would be needed again sometime soon. This matter little to the Ninja as they would be rewarded in the Hell Planes of Fire, blood and decay. They would herald in the new Ninja, the world being their hunting ground and Hell would be everyone's final destination. Lustrain began to sharpen his Shizo Katana (Large sword). He growled as the sparks flew as the sword was sharpened to unimaginable sharpness. He but lay the sword on flesh and it would slice and bite deeply into the adversary. The stone and fire that was the Demon's main meditation room was blisteringly hot but this mattered not to the Demon as he had forged himself well in the arts of Dark Ninjitsu. He had won himself with much honour the rites of Demon hood. He was once a young man when he had been entranced and seduced by the Devil Sethkis. Wha had promised him a seat at the Tengu table, only for the loyalty. He was entreated into the Nine Planes of hell and began to grow, twist and mutate into the demon he was now.

Lustrain trained hard and began to master the ways of demonic Ninjitsu. He was once the famed martial artist John Dooley. A world renowned cage fighter who's specialty was shoot fighting. He was undefeated in more than just fighting he had become adept in the ways subtlety and sabotage. Then when he was at the peak of his career the Devil made the offer to make him a powerful Tengu. He offered him everything Knowledge, women and money. But as he signed his life in the blood of the man he had to vanquish. He realised that he would never be the same. In fact the change he underwent, was twisting and agonizing. He realised way too late that he was Demon, and that he would never be able to change. No, the deal was struck and time would only enslave him all the more, oh, he was powerful, but that was only to his enemies own realization. He knew and sometimes reflected on the agonizing change, he was lost and could never change back. This had led him to crying tears of blood over his bodies hunger. His new mission was to destroy Romeo and his friends, then to go over to Japan and wipe out the old man. He had no qualms over the task but something was wrong he had a feeling of indecision, puzzlement and he did not know why. No something was wrong. He couldn't place his finger on it.

Chapter 8

Romeo was reading one of the Golden Dragons spells and copying the hand shape that was on the scroll, no he was mastering the art of Buddha fist. And the spells that came along with it. This turned out to be limitless power and affirmative action. Romeo knew he would have to read and study the Golden Dragon scrolls for many nights and days. The Buddha fist was only part of the selection that he had managed to bring back from the Jin Go realm. He had white tiger style that too had a section of magic. Also crane and snake that was full of knowledge on the healing aspect of martial arts. That particular section had been undertaken by Kikieo. The more he studded the more he was awash with the pure light and energy of martial arts. He was free of his diseased old body and the more he read the more his inner light began to shine. As did Kikieo, he smiled as he watched her complete the hand movements that led to her becoming an arcane martial master of flowers. She was noting down certain herbs and potions of strange brews that revitalized and rejuvenated the body. Certain magics that would bring a person back from death. But these came with a strong warning, that the spell drained a lot of energy from the caster. Sometimes and it had been known that the spell had killed both caster and survivor. She carried on reading and realised it was depending on the time and how long the corpse had been left the longer the more chance for it being useless. And thus dangerous for the caster. They were engrossed in the writings of the Arcane and holy words of the Golden Dragon order. This was a blessing in all parts for the Ninja and Mata Hari.

Meanwhile Giros was looking into the lore on the Tengu, figuring if he found out the name of the demon he could be restrained and rendered useless. But this was an arduous task. And they had never even set sight on the demon, much less learned its name. But they knew that it was hunting them. And needed all the information they could get. They also needed to renew their skills, hone them, sharpen up their instincts and become more than just man, become spirit, become true Shinobi. And if one thing was for sure they would need every blessing they could get. And even then they knew that this was a demon straight from hell.

They had all been tutored in the art form of Ninjitsu. But this was going to take all their power, all their strength and it was even more deadly the supernatural powers that the Tengu seemed to employ to raise the dead, the mists of time, a confusing mist that beguiled and confused the people in its confines. Leading the Ninja and their group into hazardous climates searing heat, icy cold and chaotic winds. This was but a part of its powers, no the Tengu were known for mirror images and much, much, more. It was going to take all their skills to vanquish the Tengu. They carried on their studies. This studious time lasted several weeks, and even then it was far from complete. The night sailed in to the break of dawn and the arduous task was nearly finished. They could only pray they had enough time to put the spells into action. And that meant they had to familiarize with the sacred symbols and various Incantations and also the shadow shapes that protected them from destroying their use.

They were sealed in the ancient shadows of dragons and they knew little about the dragons as well, as they hadn't been seen on earth since the dinosaur ages. But something spiritual kept them from ditching the whole idea. No, they had tasted the fruit of knowledge and now they wanted more. Things changed for the four Shinobi they had become resilient to the fear that had somehow followed them in the Jin Go realm. No, they had only a short while in which they had to train and study. But they had managed to do so competently and with a degree of skill. They were in a state of studios bliss a Nirvana that you only attained when you were called upon. They knew the value of each other and they knew how to work with each other. They had made a claim to the spirit of the Golden Dragon. And thus they had produced a lively way in which they could use the skills. No they had lived and breathed in the dragon and its essence, everything that felt natural was a rite of the dragon's scroll. They had made the shadow of the dragon and made it well. It coursed through the veins, it pumped in the meridians of the four of them, it also grew in strength the more it was studied, the more it's essence joined in molecular harmony (or spirit).

They knew they were blessed and that was a godsend, though God would be sitting this one out. As he was sure that these pupils of the Dragon were hardy enough and they were ready for the Tengu and its six demon curses. They thought carefully about the six demon curses and put into play the divine golden shadow. A part of the dragon that was going to really strengthen their resolve, show them things that they needed shown. And they were strong in the action of martial arts. The weapons the hand to hand skill this was all the blessings they needed. The spells were of arcane nature and very hard to get right. So practice, practice, practice, was all they could do. They were familiarising themselves with the sacred arcane hand shapes and verbal words as they threw a small token on the ground. Usually made of wood or stone. They placed a lot of empathises on the components of their spells. This was because talk was cheap. And anyone can hear someone mutter a word, but few placed a price on the words of sorcery especially with the component being a rare metal or unusual herb that had died out decades before. No they were blessed in the fact that descriptions of said herbs and where abouts of mineral deposits were included in the scrolls. They were also in the scrolls diagrams of demonic pressure points that had been passed down from centuries of fighting and studying the Tengu.

Chapter 9

Jason was studying said points when Romeo came into the study hall. Where Jason was tossing shurikens at the vital points of a dummy nine feet off the floor, it was only by sheer studious that Jason had discovered fifteen death points. These were all good and said but he had very little operational workings of said points.

Romeo smiled "How you doing with the points?" He asked.

Jason sniffed as if this was going to be a long conversation, "The points usually need using in a number of different ways, the fact is you need to hit three or four different points in under a minute for their full use".

Romeo looked hard and fast at the points that were hit by Jason. "But that doesn't mean you will get a favourable result. Mostly you paralyse the demon. Then…" And he threw a shuken into one of the points near the caratid vein, then he threw three others at various points on the chest.

"But I'm still no further forward, if that will actually work, or it may just paralyze the demon".

Romeo nodded his head as Jason went on about several more possibilities. But Romeo made a mental note of said points.

He then approached Kikieo who was reading an ancient scroll pertaining to the help of herbs and mystical massage points that the Golden Dragon had guarded for centuries. Very few of these points were available to the average person and few of the techniques were used these days. But she was making progress with acupuncture and sword fingers placing energy and circling the Hara and the various chakra's. She was getting good at easing pressure and keeping the four of them from exhausting themselves. While they were conducting themselves in such a demanding and exhausting task. She made Ginseng tea and released pressure from each of them and this kept the four of them from collapsing from the pressure of studies. It was six more days until the Japanese moon of the hunt a mid-winter solstice, in which they were blessed and brought forth the greatest fighters in the village to be challenged and the victor got the spoil (Usually the princess of the local province). But in the present it was just a martial arts tournament.

With the local dojo's and schools placing bets on the fighting styles of their pupils. This was where Lustran was going to begin his quest on the four Shinobi, hopefully all being to plan he would wipe out the four of them as combatants. He was smiling as he brought forth his best fighter. The young Jujitsu fighter was born and bred Japanese and had seldom lost a fight. He was going straight into the professional circuit that was just outside Nagoya. Lustran smiled as the fighter, Haru, made the grappler knot on his used black belt. The knot was full and taught and the eyes of the Grappler were green and cloudy. As if a milky white film had lain over his bright green eyes. But he could see as well as any-one.

Haru walked the short distance to the cage in which Jason stood stretching and easing the knots out of his tendons. He was ready for anything, the two combatants began to size each other up and began to throw kicks and punches. Some landed some missed and others were blocked by the recipient. Then the two of them began to close the guard on each other, hoping for a good solid choke hold. They both closed the ground and began to try triangles and chokes. Jason was in trouble for a short while, but escaped the triangle that he had gotten himself in. He began to pound and ground the Jap who was on equal footing with the small Jap. And was letting of a barrage of punches whilst straddling the Young Jap Haru.

The Jap was well in tune when the bell rang. Jason stepped off the Jap who was a bit wounded but not enough to put him out the match. The Referee sent the two of them to their respective corners. And Jason kept on bouncing on his feet knowing that this was not as easy as he had anticipated. The Japanese man, Haru, seemed to have boundless energy. And it looked like he was in full control of the fight. Jason spat his water then pushed the gumshield back in to his mouth. They clashed again in the centre of the Octagon. They began to grip each other and take the fight to the floor. It looked like it was anyone's fight as the fighters began to get busy with neither of them getting an advantage. No they couldn't seem to get a choke hold or a striking advantage. They coiled round each other like two cobras in the jungle. But neither of them could get an advantage. Their hard earned attempts of weakening each other's guard was just not paying off. They were mounting each other and throwing a few ground and pound. But there were both blocking and defending from the attacks. Haru managed to smash into Jason's ribs who took the blows and showed no sign of pain. No he was a seasoned pro but Haru was fighting with supernatural abilities. He rolled out of another great clinch and choke by Jason. And Jason shook his head as the bell went again. They separated and went to their corners.

Romeo smiled and said to Jason, "Keep it up, do not relent. Pound and pound him that's the only way you are going to win keep him down".

Jason nodded to Romeo, Giros looked at the young Jap and wondered where he was getting the energy. Then he saw his eye's and said, "The fucker is possessed".

Romeo looked at the Jap and said, "Yup, he's part demon alright".

Jason sighed and said, "That means nothing, he's still human".

Romeo cupped the back of Jasons neck. "You'll just have to fight twice as hard to win".

It was the young Japs eyes, they were maddening and well, insane. But at the same time he was calm in demeanour, and still had what looked like a tonne of energy. Romeo smiled and put the mouthpiece back into Jasons mouth. He began to bounce again. Then the bell went. And the Jap went straight at him. Starting with a spinning back kick. It connected but Jason was ready for anything. Jason returned with a front sweep and swooping grapple. He had him down and pushed him into the cage. And again he was on top, ground and pound. Smashing into Haru.

The bell rang and rang but Jason wasn't finished the referee pulled him off. And Jason smiled as the young Jap lay there dizzy and concussed from the barrage of punches he had taken. Jason pushed his hands into the air as he was announced the victor. But he hadn't won easily, as the punches he had taken from the young Jap had broken a number of ribs. But Jason had been hit worse, Jason couldn't really feel the pain, he knew he would be sore in the morning. He went into the dressing rooms where Romeo and Giros patched him up and said, "That was close".

Jason looked at Romeo as he said this. "Too close," was the reply from Jason. Then Giros put a warm sponge to the back of his neck to ease the tension from a choke hold that he had suffered. But Jason was a man of fighting spirit, and had a smile on his face as they took the cage fighting gloves off. He had never been defeated in the cage. And he had struggled just to get to the right weight for certain matches.

Chapter 10

Lustran growled as the inept warrior was walked through to the changing rooms on his side of the Octagon. He sat down as the large Tengu waved the rest of his Ninja away.

"You could have done better,#."

Haru gulped and said, "Yes Master"

Then the Tengu smiled as the young Jap took off his gloves "I'm tired of this," Said Lustran.

The young Jap was prepared for some sort of punishment, but what he didn't know. The large Tengu Demon was giving him a second chance. And knew full and well that he would need all his soldiers. "I'll forgive it this once. But if you fail me again I'll dine on your fresh corpse, after bleeding you dry for my wine." He then walked back into the shadows he had come from and vanished into the night air.

*

Romeo and the rest of them headed back to the Tiger Dojo's in the area of Nagoya. Sporting a new belt that had been won honourably so. The old Shidoshi greeted them as they arrived.

"Ah Romeo, ah Jason, ah my most treasured two students".

Romeo began to recollect the last time he had visited the Tiger Dojo's they had some trouble with the Lin Qua. This had escalated and turned into a massacre. In which his Grandson Shuzi and the rest of his clan had been brutally murdered at the hands of the Lin Qua. They had been cut down like wheat it took weeks to clean the bamboo mats. This was why only the four Shinobi were left to fight the Lin qua. But Romeo had turned the tables and found out that the real traitor was his Sensei. Who had competently managed to face the Lin Qua and the Koga off. He was a slippery character and it was at the Pinnacle of his power, but Giros had split his kidneys with his weapon of choice Sai.

Jason hadn't joined the fight until the end when they had to destroy a band of motorcycle thugs The Dark Fang. But they had done this and done it well, it was rivers of viscose blood flowing down into the streets. And the Hell's Angel were finished. Just before the final strike was done they had seen to the demise of the Lin Qua with the help of a police lieutenant Carl Rolson who had managed to get a small strike force of Chinese Gung fu, hard hitting police officers. This had really tipped the balance. But they had still yet to find the rogue demon of a Ninja called Brian Mcarthy. But Romeo knew that now that he was back Brian would want to finish off Romeo. But Romeo was confident that next time they clashed Romeo would see to the demise of the ghost-like Brian Mcarthy. He had mortally wounded Romeo the last time, but this time Romeo was at full strength and totally fearless. They all conversed for several hours and drank Japanese green tea. Then they all respectively went to their futons and slept.

The morning came and the five Ninja all woke refreshed and ready to take on a new day. It was a warm day with the sun rising warmly and breathing the life of a new spring onto them. They spent another seven days practicing and studying. It was warming and nice to hear the Kia's and soft Qui sounds as they practiced their dark arts. They were training and training hard. Sometimes the soft art of Tai Chi other times Tai Jitsu. They practiced the shadow hand discipline as well. A way to beguile and confuse even the most deadly of enemies. They knew that what they were facing was a supernatural force something that they had only heard of. They continued with their studies, Jason carried on showing the rest of them the weak points on the Tengu. He had dived right into the studies and showed great aptitude in the way of learning the ways of the Tengu It's strengths and weaknesses. What to avoid and what to focus on.

He was careful in his examination of the Tengu, as it's chi was like no mortal, yet it had come from a mortal man. Had shaped itself in the very pits of hell. Become the monstrous creature that all martial artists feared. A true Tengu Demon. Its blackened nails its sharpened teeth. Its thirst for blood it's hunger for human meat. Its way to survive and stalk the very living souls of those that it had been sent to destroy. It was a demon of the highest order. There were others, but none had the strength and constitution that Lustran was imbibed with. He had become a true demon and shaped the fates of those that were destined to be a part of its hunger. His completion of tasks on those holy and benevolent. And those malicious who were to be punished didn't last long either. Some he tortured for days others a quick clean kill. But they all knew when facing the Tengu Lustran that they had slipped into the demon's hands of fate. His martial arts skill was known as the Hands of Fate and he was undefeated. With years of study and years of practice he had become a deliverer of death. And he loved to punish the good and the weak. But this was not without its restraints. He only did what was asked of him by a greater devil. And his master Sethkiss. Serpent Lord and a true greater Devil.

He had commanded the Arcane evil minions to rebel against the holy and the righteous. To sack the holy temples of the gods and dine on the flesh of man and creature. Of divinity. This happened the world over, Asia, Africa, Europe, Indo China. The Celtic and the faraway lands of Japan had produced a mighty rise of heroic and strong will of nature. They threw down their enemies and destroyed as many of the demons as they could, this was the nature of things. And hope seemed at hand during these dark ages. Ninja and various other martial arts threw down their shackles and destroyed the Demonic reign. The world slipped the noose that had been resting on the Holy and beloved earth. The Lord again smiled at the humans knowing that man would have to be its own saviour. It was the only time Japan welcomed in the Scottish Barbarin. (Gaijin).

The Scottish helped and aided the Japanese who knew that their folk tales were just as romanticised as theirs. A force of several kilted men and several Ninja got together and fathomed out ways to fight the Demonic oppression. And how to hold sway with their rights to the Heavenly kingdoms of both Japan and Scotland. This war raged on even to this day. It was just a minor headache to the locals as the thought the martial arts code had died years ago, yet still they watched martial arts tournaments. They still routed for the Brazilian Jujitsu master who was half the size of the opponents. If they knew why the world was entrusted to several shoguns and many clans in the Celtic lands, they would hand in their sons and daughters and beg for the sacred training in the Golden Dragons rites. But very few people believed. And fewer people wanted trained. Thinking that everything was alright in the Earth. And that they had no reason for faith or martial arts and the magic that went hand and hand with it.

They didn't believe that nature was made up of both negative and positive furies. The thought we were just naked apes and they believed that nothing magical could be alive in this plane of existence. They were wrong and years of legends had been forgotten and that the poverty of Christ was just made up to be a teaching a do unto others thing. And the whole demon and devil thing was just a way to control our society. No such thing as magic tell that to the Monks of China and the other Asian lands. The whole battle for the righteous was seen as nonsense by most. But it is being fought on all fronts not just against poverty but slave drivers and sexual predators. Some say they are the ones truly lost others well others say no good without evil. These were the truly lost the ones that had wandered from the beaten path. Knowing that salvation was just a word for putting your hand in your pocket. Help those souls

Help those souls.

Chapter 11

The five Shinobi enjoyed a pleasant stay in the halls of the Koga, but knew that this was just the eye of the storm. A lull that had come just to set them in their place. On the eighth night they experienced a small battle. The Tengu had sent a little force of Demonic Ninjas to chip away at their resources. It was a five man mission that was what the Tengu thought was fair, considering the fact that one of them was an elder. But knew that this didn't matter as the oldest of men had faced a lot more of lives challenges. And were that little bit wiser. That little more dangerous and had every trick in the book under wraps and that meant that they were more cunning more resilient. No, the Old Shidoshi had nearly a hundred years of experience. And was as crafty as a man could be, he knew ways to kill a man painfully and ways to kill a man quietly. And everything else was a bonus.

He slipped into the shadows of the Koga Dojo's. As did the rest of them, all except Romeo, no he lay, pretending to be sleeping. The other hooded and armed to the teeth waited as the five Tengu Ninja began to circle the so called sleeping form of Romeo who again was dressed in the Koga Tiger Gi. They carried on circling with their weapons held steady and ready, then the old Shidoshi gripped on of them suddenly dragged him into the shadows and pierced his heart with a Ninja dagger, killing the Tengu straight away. The other four realised but realised too late it was a trap. Giros flipped through the air and came face to face with one of them. He circled his Katana and sliced at the Tengus neck, the blade bit and bit deeply. The blood gushed down the front of the Tengus body, he had cut the Tengus windpipe. Romeo was seeing to one of the last three Tengus with his weapon of choice Kama, he was parrying and striking out at the Tengu. But wasn't getting near enough for a lethal strike.

Jason grabbed one of them and Kikieo did the same almost simultaneously. They both disposed of the Tengu with surety and ferocity. Each giving a Kia (Spirit shout) When they finished the two Tengu. Romeo was backing the other Ninja towards the stairwell. He got to the top and Romeo decided to use the fact he was out on a limb to his advantage. He rolled and sliced as he got close enough to the Tengu sending him tumbling down the stairs at which point he broke his neck. Then the bodies suddenly were engulfed in green flame and they vanished back to the Pits of hell.

They re-grouped and removed their hoods. And sat and had some tea. The acrid tea was refreshing and rejuvenating. It hit the spot. They went straight back to their studies. They knew that the Demon would not be pleased with his loss of Ninja. But was just going to have to accept it. He would bide his time and wait for a better way to kill his quarry. He had all the time in the world. But knew they were studying the Arcane of the Golden Dragon order. He wouldn't rush them that was sure. Then he smiled as he watched through a seeing fire at the Five Shinobi as they practiced day and night seemingly un perturbed by the little fight they had just had. Then he had an idea, "Brian Mcarthy". He said out loudly knowing that he and his school of Ninja would be helpful in the destruction of the five Shinobi.

"A mere pawn with such destructive powers, Yes Lustran it is a wise move". Came the words from Sethkis, a telepathic link that his Devil Master had with Lustran.

"Thank you, Master," came the gravelly voice of Lustran. "I shall deal with this personally". He then sent word to Brian Mcarthy, that an old Ninja sect would like to offer him a chance to revitalise a truce and the merging of both their schools. They now just had to wait for the Ghost-like Ninja to return his invitation with either a yes or no. But this would take a while. And Lustran who had a quick temper was seething with anger and knew there was nothing he could do but wait.

*

Romeo was on the phone to an old acquaintance. A fellow martial artist who had been there when the death of Julie really angered and sent Romeos spirits reeling.

"I need to meet with you have you look at a few old scrolls that are in my possession". The man whose name was Christian Gibs, who was a killer Jujitsu and Judo fighter and also a man of arcane knowledge when it came to the Jin Go realm, he knew his stuff.

Christian laughed and said, "I thought you were dead?".

Romeo joined in the laughter and replied, "It would appear I am back and I got a hold of a shit load of stuff from one of the Jin Go Temples the Golden Dragon sect."

Christian Gibs laughed some more and said, "I doubt you have got the genuine Golden Dragon scrolls as they were burned years ago in a shaolin monastery fire".

Romeo sighed as if the statement was true but he had neither the time nor the energy to converse over the phone.

"I'll be over in a day or two," said Christian.

Romeo hung up the phone and went back to his practice. He knew these studies would aid him in what every Martial artist called it 'the Demon Wars'. It was strange, but everyone in the martial arts community had a creeping fear that was chilling their very blood. And that fear was becoming more and more powerful, and the cause of the creeping fear was Lustran. Demonic duke, a creature who had come from the humble ranks of martial prowess to the power and sinister malignant surge of evil. He was regarded with respect in the demonic underworld. He had proved himself a mighty weapon that had honed itself into the evil embodiment that every martial artist had come to fear. It was known amongst them they would fall upon their own swords in the terror and retribution. But also their was whispers that Romeo would be the saviour in the martial arts community. But some sneered and said that he was more fictitious than the Demon from the Pits of Hell. No, some laughed others were taken to long days and nights of meditation.

Preparing themselves for the rift between the positive side of the dao and the negative side. They equal and level pegging. But it was a bad rift with those of the shadow going to the dark side whilst those of good, were trusting in the light of truth. And hoping to win in the said clash between good and evil. Romeo knew one thing that the fight had started thousands of years ago. The ancient oriental gods of light and true wisdom, were still shining in the world of martial arts. Romeo was coming into bloom in the shadows of both master and student. His training had started off in the vein and terrible actions of someone who had revenge deep into his blood and soul. His double headed dragon was still tattooed onto his body. But the image had come to remind him of his strength and how much he could adapt to. How he could push further and further into the Jin Go world and survive its tests master its lessons become what he was turning out to be a martial arts saviour and protector. But this was not an easy task no there were many hazards to contend with many tests by both good and evil in the world of martial arts. They would welcome the light but also find comfort in the shadows. Givin in time they would be able to seal the Hell abominations back in the dark fiery pits. This would take all their strength and energy and sometimes it would seem impossible. Other times they would have guides, angels both Oriental and Caucasian.

Chapter 12

Christian Gibs arrived late on two days hence, He smiled as he bowed to the other four martial artists He looked at them with a smile in his eyes.

"So Romeo, where are these scrolls, and remember I know authenticity?" The question made Romeo nod and show the way to arcane arts room.

Christian looked at the binding of what was possibly forty thousand years old and had been dipped in the blood of a dying golden dragon who was one of the last to leave this world. He had given his life to honourably protect the secrets of the Jin Go world. He breathed out as he put his hands on the what would have been the greatest find of any archaeologist.

"Okay Romeo you got me interested". The statement settled into Romeo who smiled and shook his hand.

"Told you". He said

Christian smiled and shook his hand back, "We need help, some of the text is well, a bit rich".

"Christian, It's hardly surprising, probably written in dragon tongue and I suppose you know that speech?" Romeo smiled as he asked the question.

Christian washed his hand and found the small golden glow that was thrown off the scrolls grew brighter the more he read and digested. He got to the language of the Dragon and started to click and speak faintly knowing that to wake the dragon would be calamity for them all. The young arcane martial arts teacher was fascinated with the apparent boundless lessons that the scrolls spoke, thoughts within thoughts, a timeless river of power that was only needed in great times of war. He breathed out in elation. Fascinated by each scroll. He was enthralled by the sheer power of the scrolls as after each lesson there was a continuation of a former lesson where he had to pick up and the scrolls would tell of not only hand and body training, but of mental training, training that taught the user how to control with Psionics. The power of the mind. As it was the most valuable weapon a martial artist had, vast and destructive. Like walking through walls disappearing into mirrors. It was what he thought were just tricks. But the mind controlled the execution of that Psionics and these things were doubly useful. In the fact that the impossible was made possible and the power of the mind could and would show the way to peace, even through the hardest of battles, battles in which both sides had perished. And the true masters were the ones with the most knowledge. They had kept the dragon as a slave for some time but the dragon had freed himself many times. Many, many, many, times. He had turned into a blessed virgin and seduced the local shogun out of his wits, showing him pleasures and turning up to his house for a number of nights, spying and setting the bait. Then he vanished and let slip a parchment of all the weaknesses that could be exploited and two days later was assassinated from within. The dragon rested easy as the Shogun had been preparing to storm the Monastery where he was housed. But like it said in the old Dragon tongue, "This would have been perilous for the whole Oriental and Asian lands"

He then rested for two, three hundred years. Knowing that his power was ultimate in that victory. He had struck a blow for the martial artists in the world. He had come to know various enemies as he matured, and was taken secretly from land to land. From various temples and Buddhist shrines. These scrolls were authentic and Christian was well was overwhelmed by the sheer lessons that each of the ten scrolls taught. He called on Romeo and showed him one skill that he was really overwhelmed with and that was the 'Chanters Ear' It was a small easy spell to use and when the victim of the three sounds heard it they woke the next morning and ran straight into insanity. It was powerful and seldom used. Its secrets lay in the hot airy breath that was blown into the ear of the victim. But like I said, it was seldom used, as the effects were powerful and the results had all kinds of catastrophic ends. The most notable was the suicide that the person made after committing a savage set of deeds like killing everyone in the room as they slept. It was only natural that the Dragon had really strong reservations on the use of the spell. But there were more. There was a flame strike that you could summon and use as an offensive, it included the use of oil and tinder. Then tossing it forth whilst saying the ancient Kanji word for fire. Then he began to read the Psionic abilities like reading minds. And levitating objects whilst staying motionless.

The user of Psionics had to be a man of a certain Intellect. And very strong willed. If he or she wasn't then the power of the mind would be left to turn infantile, and the energy it thought He/she controlled would be sapped out and the strength turn on them, leaving weakness and even death. Very few had managed to control the power of dragon mindfulness. And the ones that did were worshipped like gods. Christian read on, clicking and saying the Dragon tongue out loud and placing the hands in various places and shape shifting the fingers in the five elements. This combined with Dragon speak was really lifting the fog off the rest of the scrolls. Showing Alchemy and sacred wisdom.

Romeo looked on as the Arcane martial artist spoke and translated the scrolls. The ancient times that the scrolls had travelled showed not on the text as they were preserved in the blood of the dragon. This in itself had amazed the Martial artist, Christian went deeper and deeper into the way of the Dragon. He was becoming more and more intrigued. It was a simple thing that made sense as lesson appeared and then vanished into the mind's eye. There were lessons in pictures and slow symbols that when followed to the letter imbibed the reader spells of great powers. The opening into the spirit worlds how to vanish how run with such haste that the caster was invisible apart from the slight rush of wind. He was fascinated by the scrolls, which brought upon himself instantly a certain amount of power of mindfulness with the power to confuse and beguile the weak-minded servants of evil. He was enthralled and addicted to the powerful writings by various masters who had served under the Golden Dragons powers. This studying went on for a good week and three days. Romeo took him food and tea to keep him in full energy, and he carried on studying with very little sleep and the scrolls held spells and martial arts movements that included flying and stepping like the wind through the tallest of trees. He found it more and more fascinating. He was drawing back through the end of the last two scrolls when the wisdom of such magic sent him all the way back to the beginning of the scrolls and began in the way of subtlety to teach another way for martial prowess. Intrigued, no spellbound, he couldn't get more spirit or satisfaction. Even an opium addict with freedom to as much as he wished was not as addicted as him. He was enthralled with the lessons that the scrolls taught. He went back to the first scroll several times, every time finding a new path, a new lesson. It was spiritually awakening. Christian was in his element. He stopped only to either eat or explain some of the dragons text. He even elaborated on a few of the finer points. Certain moves that had been prohibited, he smiled and showed said move to Romeo and his cohorts. It was a power strike that had been used but this one had a slight twist, it sent the advisory into a state of seizure. This in turn, if wasn't treated right away, could cause paralysis, even death a painful one at that. He carried on studying. Romeo smiled as he came to an end of his studying.

"Told ya!" He said, as Christian drew the last symbol on the last scroll. He had summoned at one point an air entity. That had shown him strength yet a little subtlety. It was answering questions that Romeo and the rest of them needed to know. Like how strong Lustran was. Where did Lustran draw his powers? What are Lustran's vulnerabilities? The entity laughed as the questions were asked he answered them carefully it's voice a whisper, almost musical.

"He has the strength of ten men".

Romeo and the rest carried on listening.

"He draws his powers from the depths of hell, to be precise the Hell of the Horned black dragon." It then gave a little breeze that cooled the air "You are on the right path to finding his weaknesses. Master Kendricks.

The entity having been used accordingly vanished. The Ninja knew all too well that, that was a powerful Guardian and that they would need it later on. The benevolent spirit was watching over them. They could feel it sometimes, hear its breathing as it circled the room making its presence known. It was a guider, a shower of truths and a powerful ally. It was certain that they would succumb to the tests that dragon scroll had begun to set them the second they had unravelled the first scroll, everything has some sort of price.

Nothing that was worth anything would come free no they had to show the dragon they were in it with strength, with cunning and with free will. They were blessed with the scrolls and knew that they were lucky to have them. They carried on their studies and Christian began to impart the lessons that were a part of the way. They began to use the spirit of the dragon, as Christian explained and showed various techniques and various forces, how to use the very nature of things, the air the rain even the lightning. Also unleash the power of the mind. Read minds see through disguises, penetrate the darkest regions of hell with holy light.

Empower their Nen Riki. Summon flame and wind. Powerful spells and powerful psionics. They were finally ready to face the Tengu Demon and his minions. It was going to get very, very ugly. The powers that were imbibed onto them was limitless and so they had to take their time. And succumb to the art of the Golden Dragon. It was difficult for a mere mortal, hell it was difficult for a spirit, the compound spells the psionics if not hindered, too could drive a man into the path of a psychotic storm, no they were going to have to take their time. Tread carefully, and hope they had got the lessons right. If they didn't and had not adhered to the rules about psionic combat they would be driven insane then left to come down from the heights of madness, this was no easy task so it was undertaken with great care and diligence. They each had mapped before them a set of dragon words and mystical shapes that had to be made at the same time. They each had four spells and two psionic mental attributes. The rest would be saved for later. They were relieved as they drew the last of their energy into themselves then settled at zen the minds calmest point.

Chapter 13

Lustran could sense and feel the Ninja, studying something that he had mercifully forgotten all about. He laughed at the winds and a bellow of smoke belched forth and out of his dominion. They were making weapons of dark and dreadful purpose. Envenomed with the poison of a thousand dead tortured souls. The blackest of magic and witchcraft folded into the blades of dark magic. Lustran's smile curved off his elongated canine teeth, He was hungry for blood and fire death and destruction, evil's only purpose is to destroy and leave nothing other than chaos, He was firing up his mind and imbibing the very spirits of hell into the recesses of his soul and brain. He began to meditate and concentrated on the field of battle. His purpose, the purpose to serve hell and all its masters this came first. He would think of a strategy. A way to lure the five Ninja into his territory where he would beguile and confuse his quarry. Then when they thought they had survived he would close each of their souls in his fist and send them into Hell. Then he would gather forth the legions of doom and destroy Earth.

He thought on and on until he had clarity of vision and the vices of hell at his command. He began to laugh as he saw out of his dominion and into the night air of Japan. He began to scheme and plan and make ready the tools at his disposal. He sent forth a team of his death's head Ninja. He sent them after Romeo and the rest of his gallant heroes. Lustran laughed some more. Then with the wave of his hand he sent his best. But this was already anticipated by Romeo. And they clashed with the deadly Ninja in a zen garden that had started to bloom. They got into the garden and instantly began to form a circle. Then they drew their weapons and started to concentrate, so as not confuse themselves in case there were too many. Romeo drew out a Kama, Jason drew his katana. The Old Shidoshi drew a katana and Tanto (Dagger). Giro unclasped his hand and several shuriken appeared ready to throw. Kikieo produced a slender sai. And Christian was holding a Jo staff. They waited and watched, it fell into a deathly silence and they knew that was trouble. They continued to concentrate.

Then out of nowhere and flying straight at Romeo came razor sharp black shuriken, he ducked and sliced his kama into the night, blocking the dark death stars. Each one was poisoned but that was a mute, point as Romeo was focused and knew that this was just the start of the battle. Jason, Iron armed his Katana and began to run into the tall conifers that surrounded the five of them. He scaled a tree and began to scan around looking for shadow traces. Romeo and the rest of them decided to engage the enemy on their terms. There were at least fifty of the Demons and Romeo was happy to fight each one. He rounded a small clearing deep into the zen garden and forest. He sighed made the mystical symbol that mirrored his image, into seven of him then they split off and went different ways. Leading the demons into a trap. Were the seven images conversed in to one and he was knelt as the images brought his enemy to him. He folded his fingers into Kuji and whispered Retsu then he vanished as the already confused Demons came upon the clearing. There were a good fifteen of them but that number was about to decrease. Romeo cut into two of them in two flashing slices that one went across one of their midriff. The other took of the other's head. Then blink, he vanished again. They then formed a circle they had never expected this. Romeo was concentrating on his next move when Giro's came back flipping into the clearing and straight at the group of Tengu. He then rolled straight at them and as he did this he threw with deadly accuracy his shuken. He felled four in one roll. Then Romeo blinked again and flew into the heart of the Tengu's circle, he quickly gripped one and stretched his right kama across the nearest Tengu's neck. The blood fell like a waterfall but black and viscous.

They lost morale and did the worst thing yet and that was panic. They hadn't expected on Romeo and the rest of them to have these innate abilities. They knew they had just lost the battle. Jason was striking and killing the ones as they headed towards the clearing. Their numbers began to dwindle. It was fifty, but after a while with all five of the Ninja picking them off they lost all ideas of winning and began to try and run back to where they had come, Hell. The demon Ninja arrived back into Hell. But were not greeted with victory, no, Lustran started to wade into them. His massive muscular body slicing and breaking the last of them, he then began to dine on their flesh they would have been better to die in the garden as they would have been shown more mercy. As souls and spirits of demons. No the ones that escaped Romeo and his allies died painful bloody deaths.

Romeo and the rest of his band went back to the Koga Dojos to rest. They knew they would need it as they had just angered a Devil in Hell. The zen garden was awash with demon blood but they knew it would be taken care of. As all holy and divine were rooting for them. The Jin Go world was at peace for the time being. Romeo liked his new found abilities, they all did. They slept until mid-morning then awoke refreshed and revitalised. They smiled at the morning dumplings and rice balls that they ate. They began to joke and laugh at the easiness of the battle that they had just survived. Romeo was distant as the rest of them celebrated. He knew something was amiss. It was too easy way to easy. They barely broke sweat. And finished with professional timing, knowing each other and knowing what each of them were capable of. They made a lethal strike force and Romeo smiled at this, a small confident smile. He was becoming more and more agile and confident, the Dragon magic was truly pumping through him empowering him. Making him a harder than steel person, he was truly a dragon master. But then so were they all. They carried on eating and celebrating.

Having ate33 heartily and rested comfortably. They began to meditate again each of them in half lotus and breathing calmly. They began to work their fingers into sacred knots and fist grips. Every now and then one of them would flick a sword finger at lightning-fast speed. Then murmur out a power word. Then draw a zen, then back to finger knitting. Fire, wood, Chi, then earth, as they cast the shapely spells. Then metal into each of their spirits. This was again sealed with a zen master's sign. Then another quick sword finger drawing the symbol of water. They carried this on until late into the night. The five of them held a fierce and dangerous power and knew that it wouldn't let them down, but it could be used against them so Christian took the duty to hold and protect the scrolls.

He was honoured to do so, and Romeo knew that he and the rest of them were in good hands whilst Christian, showed them more and more. Untangled the web of consciousness, showed them the right path the very seeds of intelligence were sown and watered carefully to show them the right way. To become a part of them. Their spirits and will forging in the vast light of Dragon knowledge. Their bodies being shaped as iron and steel. To make their weapons more than just forged but imbibed with supernatural fires and magic. They began to rest and let their bodies be awash with the powers of the Golden dragon. Their minds were empty yet full of light their bodies were relaxed yet ready to strike. Romeo began to flow into a small set that he had been working on one of the Dragons sacred movements. Christian watched as the spirits flowed through Romeo. He was more than powerful he was supernatural and flowed and twisted into moves that hadn't been seen in thousands of years. He finished with a crane blow. The rest who were in a deep meditated trance, came to and watched Romeo as he moved with subtlety and harmony and drew a zen calm and collected. They all smiled as the word for zen is peace.

Chapter 14

Lustran was picking his teeth with the bones on one of his lesser and inferior demons, he had to realign his evil demonic spirit and there was no other way than eating and sleeping. He had a smile on his face that was twisted and sinister. And he was guiding his thoughts and energies into an evil scheme, a path of deadly evil, he was in fact summoning evil dark magic and sending his senses out onto the dank cold wind. He then got close enough to the group of Ninja so as he could hear them murmuring. The evil flesh he had eaten was still settling in his guts. But he knew he was on the right course as their aura and chakras were aligning. He would wait another day and night then he would strike with the evil that he had summoned into himself. He readied and lay still as they started to do the Kuji Kirri again. He began to chant, to himself and he was tying lightning around his fist then he entered the Old Shidoshi who felt the pain in his chest first, then he floated up from his half lotus. The Demon began to twist and destroy the old man, this went on for a number of minutes then the old man fell, as the last of his bones snapped. Romeo cried out in panic and they all rushed to the old man as he gasped and blood seeped out of his mouth as he died an agonizing death. His face was contorted and stretched in horror. They gathered round as the cold wind blew out their candles.

They just realised that they were being hunted. And not by a mere demon but all the demons in hell. They all felt the chill as the demon vacated the dojos. And went back to the Pits of Hell. Christian rested the eyes of the old man and said, "I take it that was the demon that you have to vanquish?"

Romeo sighed and his eye watered, "That was a great man".

Romeo sobbed slightly and lit some sandalwood sticks to hopefully ease the journey for the old Shidoshi. The old man entered the Jin Go world and headed straight to the Golden Dragons Monastery. He was now out of the game of survival but knew that he may be able to help in a spiritual capacity. He started his journey to the Dragon's Monastery were he would begin a vigil of meditation and fasting. He would concentrate and let the powers of the dragon grow and feed him. With knowledge and techniques. He had a very positive attitude as he got closer to the Dragon's Gates. His eyes softened as he glanced his gaze onto Romeo's other half. He smiled and looked at the young woman and said, "Beauty within Beauty".

She smiled and took his hand and led him to the arcane scroll room, as they entered the room she said, "You might be able to even things later on you just have to be prepared."

He smiled and replied, "I'm old, even my astral bones are feeling the ware of time".

She smiled and shook her head and said, "You have much to teach and also much to learn"

The Shidoshi smiled as at a small table sat the young frame of Shuzi. The old Shidoshi was overwhelmed when his gaze landed on him. Shuzi looked up from the ancient arcane tome he was studying and saw his grandfather. He smiled, lay down the Tome and ran right into his waist. The old man held him tight for a number of minutes. Then said to the young Ninja, "You really are an exceptional student".

The young boy smiled and said, "I owe it all to you Grandad". He then motioned for the old man to sit opposite him and tell him everything that had happened since he was butchered. The old man told everything, how the Lin Qua were vanquished and Romeo had finally saved face. He then told the Young Ninja about how the Togakure had planned the whole thing to claim the rights to the Opium and other Narcotic's. They're treachery knew no bounds. They then both began to read and study the various Tomes handed down from thousands of years from the day the dragon had come to be friends with the benevolent of martial artists. But only the benevolent, no one else was worthy and they knew it, as shaolin guarded the fierce dragons tomb and only let the most distinguished and patient into the tomb. Where martial artists were bathed in its mighty aura and summoned into its power. That was the ultimate lesson where they were told and filled with spells of unimaginable power. If you even had small part of darkness the spirit of the dragon would devour you and send you back into the pits of hell. Where you belonged. Shuzi had become quite the scholastic and showed even the most powerful of sorcerers how they were not paying attention and missed certain key elements. He was a keen student and knew of many different ways to approach the ancient literature. He was growing vast, in magic showing simple things then turning them into great spells of power. And his martial prowess had grown as well he had learned the dragon jade sword skill. It too was simple to Shuzi. He had completed it in a number of weeks. The old Shidoshi couldn't be more proud of his grandson. And then after a fine dine of fruit and rare vegetables he slept his first peaceful night since the death of Shuzi. He was home and honoured.

Chapter 15

Romeo was sat watching Kikieo and Giros as they sparred with their weapons of choice. Giro's had a pair of nunchucks and Kikeo had a sai. And the other hand had a tiger spike on it. They practiced played almost dreamily, with little sound or little breath. They were going into the extremities of Ninjutsu. Keeping balance whilst trading gentle blows. They moved skilfully whilst keeping the mind in check, no fear, no panic and a bright and healthy mind. It was all scholastic and trained from years of forging their spirits in the fires of martial arts. No, they were beyond minor skill, even medium skilled, no, they were in all accounts grand masters. Kikieo was a grand master of flowers, whilst Giros was a grand master of the golden dragon. They were locked in training against each other knowing that they were equal in spirit and proficiency. This training session had lasted since the break of dawn and was going strong into mid-afternoon. They were so adept that even Romeo was growing weary of watching their deadly dance. No, there was just balance and skill, they knew each other to well and Romeo stood and shouted, "Stop".

The two of them came to a halt right when the each had each other on a deadly blow. They froze then both smiled at each other. This had been the pinnacle of their art. And the day drew slowly into night. The warm weather was breaking into Japan and things became more settled Christian was still fascinated with the scrolls of the dragon and knew he couldn't take much more. The lessons were growing more and more complex. He still wasn't sleeping and still kept opening more and more ways. He knew he couldn't keep this up, he would end up the shell of a man with no spirit at all it was one of the treacherous paths that he had to keep up. He was still spell bound by the literature of the ancient golden dragon. But alarm bells were ringing and Cristian had to pry himself away, trying to gain composure and still be astute. Romeo covered him with a blanket as he lay babbling slightly in the tongue of dragon. Romeo nodded his head and said, "You truly love your work friend".

He then exited the small room and closed the door behind him.

*

Lustran smiled at the victory that he had just acquired. He was happy in the fact that he had found a way to get at the Ninjas. And that was the most satisfying part of the whole destructive force. He found that if he waited a few more days, he may get another chance at the Ninja. But something was wrong something he had overlooked. Something he had dismissed. The feeling tortured him whilst he meditated. But he wasn't going to rule out his victory. No he was pleased with it, wallowed in it, Knew that it was the first part of a treacherous plan. A plan that seemed too simple, yet diabolical in its mechanics. He was feeling the glory rush of success. He just needed to begin a new plan one that might procure him the souls of the do-gooding Ninja. This was no easy task and he knew it. He called on his most deadly servant Coltar. He came into the hall of blood and bone with a small smile on his face. "Yes master!" He said then bowed, he was half the size of Lustran and knew his place as he bowed again.

Lustran smiled and boomed "Coltar you are my most worthy of servants. I have a mission for you"

Coltar rung his hands in anticipation and his eyes gleamed of hell fire. He knew his place and knew it well. He smiled a sinister small growl. In which his lip curled showing his fangs. He listened as the greater demon told him of his new wicked and malicious plan. It was focused on either Jason Kendricks or the scholar Christian. Both of whom were important in their ways of the dragon. But no not Jason, no he was really in a mood with the scholar, he had surpassed his expectations and could be dangerous. He smiled and looked at the lesser demon. I need an assassination plan.

Coltar's voice cracked as he replied, "Who has got you questioning your superior powers master?"

Lustran gave a small laugh, "The Scholar, the man who has found out the secrets of the dragon scrolls".

Coltar bowed again and answered, "I take it he may be dangerous to the plans of you master?"

Lustran sighed as if bored with the conversation. "Do as you see fit but bring me his head"

Coltar gave a sinister chuckle and said, "Yes master this will be a walk in the park".

He then set about the task of blending into the shadows and hiding in the confines of the Koga Dojo's. He would wait as long as it took to follow the Ninja

Scholar. And if the opportunity arose he would strike. But Romeo had a psychic link into the underworld and had witnessed the conversation. He mentally watched the demon Coltar as he dressed in the blackest of robes, then disappear into the shadows. He watched and waited as Christian began to teach the rest of them the last of the secrets of the Golden Dragon.

Romeo had excused himself feeling the presence of the demon Coltar. He too vanished into the shadows and had a strong feeling of where Coltar was. So he watched the shadows as they grew and changed, as they moved following Christian, Romeo smiled into his hood. He now knew where the demon was about to strike. Just outside Christian's study room. It was the perfect plan, but Romeo had seen through it and was ready. Christian walked to the door of the study after another well taught lesson in the magics of the Golden Dragon. When Coltar struck with his blackened blade of evil, Romeo saw the strike as it came out of the shadows. And he pounced like a tiger, straight at the evil demons attack. He pushed the sword back and the demon hissed at him.

"Romeo, Romeo," he said as they began their deadly dance.

Each one of them pushing and trying to get the other of balance. Romeo was determined to take the demons life then send him back to the pits and bowers of Hell. Christian stood still as Romeo and the demon struck, parried and struck again. They were waiting for each other to make the slightest of mistakes in the battle. But neither of them got the chance. They were evenly matched. And that was that. No they had neither the cunning nor the strength to beguile each other. That's when Giros rounded the corner and struck at the demon without even giving it a second's thought. He threw three razor sharp shuriken at the demon, They struck into its flesh and gave Romeo the chance he needed. Romeo then took one of his Kama and took of the demons horned head off. Coltar was vanquished, defeated, his mistake not counting the variables. Like Giros.

*

Romeo smiled as he took the headless demons corpse out into the courtyard where a Buddhist Monk blessed the remains sending its soul straight back to Lustran. Romeo smiled and bowed to the Monk. The Monk smiled and bowed back. But the fact remained they had lost the old Shidoshi, and he would be missed in the battles to come. Romeo went back into the Koga Dojo's and rested knowing that the Tengu Demon was fast becoming aware that he wasn't facing a group of amateurs, no he was fighting seasoned Ninjas and this could only go two ways, one he would destroy the group, or two he would be destroyed.

Chapter 16

The old Shidoshi smiled as he watched the battle from the seeing room. He perked up especially when Giros had struck the demon with his death stars. He knew now that Romeo and the other four were at the peak of their strength. They would and should be more of a match to the demon. The old Shidoshi carried on with his studies of the Golden Dragon. He was busy in the thought of becoming more than mere spirit. But a spiritual force that even the devils could not believe to exist. No, the Old Shidoshi was becoming vastly more powerful. He was levitating objects with his mind, controlling things like lightning. And showing great skill in the hand-to-hand circuit. They made him a teacher of arcane ways. Grandmaster of folding lightning a way in which very few could control. Fewer still had the power to even sustain a bolt of lightning. No the old Shidoshi showed great skill and great courage. Where this path would lead him, he knew not. But one thing was for sure he would change, change into a pure spirit of Lightning. Into the Golden Dragons most feared weapon. He would be one of the few that had encompassed the great skill of lightning folding. He was truly a grandmaster. More so now he had traversed the Jin Go world and successfully tamed the dragons spirit. He knew he had a destiny to come to.

And Romeo and the rest of them would need his guidance and his help. Shuzi smiled as he sent forth a bolt of lightning at the same time as his grandad.

They had been studying together for what seemed like weeks but in fact it was only days. No he had made a breakthrough on the second day, it was a quick break through and only him and a limited number had even came close to that level of consciousness. He was surprised at how fast he had developed, the art of lightning. And Shuzi was hot on his heels and gaining more and more momentum, showing no fear in the preparation of the skill. The two made a sacred pact, that they would always be together as they shared a supernatural bond. Shuzi was a quick learner but he had been there longer. So a few things that he knew were a bit more easy for him. He had traversed the basics so quickly that even the Shaolin were impressed.

The Jin Go world seemed strange at first to the young Koga but after diluting the basics he became an adept. Tamed the dragons spirit, became more than mere Ninja. He only had one more set of lessons and they were the toughest trials going the way of the Dragon. You had to meditate for four nights and four days you had to have impeccable set routines. And then you had to traverse the Dragons cavern, deep in the bowers of the monastery. He and his grandad would take the journey were they would be washed in the fires of the Golden Dragon. Their will and souls braving the challenge of dragons fire. They would change as the heat and sheer force of the spirit of the Golden Dragon. It would shine in them and if not, it would kill them. But this challenge lay weeks away they had to master at least fourteen sets of martial prowess. They carried on showing great determination and great knowledge. They had already traversed the halls of death and succeeded, this had shown well for them, one of the shaolin masters made the comment, "The dragon is pleased with you, well done".

He then carried on with his Chin Na lessons. The old Shidoshi smiled as he continued with another complicated Kata. He finished said Kata and right at the end he aimed a bolt of lightning into the ground, using his sword fingers. This was then swiftly followed by the young Ninja Shuzi. Who did the same set and finished the same way. They were both applauded by the rest of the monks who had been brought to stop so as to watch the old man and his grandson, they had learned much.

*

Romeo and the rest of them were going over the basic spells of the golden dragon. There was much to learn and even if the learned all the scrolls there were lessons within lessons. Ways within ways. And the more Christian studied the more he learned. The power was sometimes to immense for him and he had to lay the scrolls down. But he knew that if he hadn't he could wind up dead or a vegetable babbling and talking to himself. He lay down and rested for the remainder of that day and night. Romeo kept watch and made sure he didn't lose sight of his lessons especially when the teacher was exhausted. Giros, Kendricks and Kikieo sat in half lotus each making Nenriki Shapes of the Golden dragon again every so often saying a power word. These words manifested themselves into various powers, one was a fireball the other was a small earthquake. Others were ice and invisibility.

They were learning more and more how to read minds. How to confuse and beguile even the most intelligent of beings. Mirror image was another and of course shape shifting. They knew that said powers would only last for a couple of days then they would have to re-energise themselves and go over the meditations again. They knew this only because Christian had uncovered it. It was a vital part of the dragon speak, basically it said that they couldn't take anything for granted as a time lapse always appeared. And then they would either fail in the casting or they would collapse out of sheer exhaustion. Both results took their toll on the user. So it would have to be small skirmishes then back then another small skirmish. They had to be careful because if certain things weren't done right the spell could end up losing its target and end up turning on the user. They carried on studying. Summoning the various elements. They knew that it was treacherous to even learn the way of the dragon because if it sensed you were out to use the dragon spirit out of malice or ill will, it would consume you. But so far so good. They hadn't encountered any such problems. But then they had nothing to hide.

"Have you ever seen the dragon chew someone up and spit them out?" Christian asked Romeo and the four Ninja.

Romeo and the rest of them all murmured "No!".

"It's a similar thing to what happened to the old Shidoshi. But the dragon takes its toll with furious power and furious fire." Christian carried on the count as each of them made the strange finger-locking exercise and power chant.

They made whisps of smoke in the air and drew their power to a point of Zen. Then they moved into the other Kanji shapes. Gaining more and more power and strength. Christian at first had to show them each the shapes as there were a hundred and twenty of them, each one imbibed the user a small part of power, then a twist of the finger and they were empowered. Christian was proud of the other four Ninja, but in particular Kikieo. She was transferring the powerful Kanji spirit into her very spirit. She smiled as she levitated up in half lotus, she was truly gifted. And was showing remarkable power especially with the Psionic art form. This was showing as she got into people's minds and heard what they were thinking. She had traversed the skills of Psionics easier than anyone else.

She began to glow slightly as if she was truly enlightened. She had an aura around her. She could also make her Chakras glow the colour for each of them. This also enlightened her in the Healing arts of Shen and shiatsu. She could temporally send pain away and that was a good gift. The more she travelled into the healing side the more she glowed. She was finding things easier and easier. Whilst the rest of them were learning to be truly invisible and shoot powerful energies at the enemies she was learning to strike at nerve clusters and stop chakras and smash them. Leaving the enemies to fall to the ground dead. She was also helping her fellow Ninjas remember the dark Kanji shapes by putting them into the other four's mind so they wouldn't forget (easier said than done). The new moon of spring was about to rise to the heights of heaven and they knew that the evil malicious force of Lustran was low in power and this was one of the chances that they had to take at going into Hell and destroying the evil Tengu Demon. But this, as you might think, is easier said than done. Romeo was working on a small spell called summon shadows. This made you and your friends seem as if there was an army of you. But the spells major flaw was the fact it didn't last more than ten minutes.

Chapter 17

Lustran was still enjoying his victory over the group of Ninja. But he too knew of the spring moon and the kind of power it offered the benevolent force. He was comfortable in the fact they wouldn't walk into all Hell. But that was exactly what they were planning on doing. They had done enough Arcane training to fill a small army, and they were itching to use their gifts, and powers. They knew they had all the will to destroy this demon. And anyone else that would be a problem for them. It wasn't going to be easy. And, Lustran would have all the malevolent powers of Hell. Romeo smiled, as once again he donned the chain mail gauntlets and drew out the razor sharp shuriken. He had plenty and they wouldn't be a hindrance. He also put two Kama beneath his golden sash. Giros sharpened his Katana and pushed two Sai beneath his sash that was crimson. Jason smiled as he brought forth a long-weighted chain called a Mariki Gusari. He was truly exceptional with that weapon and knew exactly how to use it to its fullest potential. Kikieo donned her grey Gi and put one hand through her tiger claws and had a tanto in the other. She was undeniably exceptional with both. She would guard the rear. Because sure Hell's full of wicked souls they would try and strike them from the back. Her part in this was much needed. Christian on the other hand was going in empty hand. No weapons just his fist and feet. He was prepared to die. It would be an honourable death but if the fates stayed with them it would be an honourable victory. He was happy with either.

*

Meanwhile the old Shidoshi and Shuzi were finishing off their studies and preparing to walk into the lair where the dragon had come to rest. They bound their hands and bound their feet as they knew that it was an arduous task and even more treacherous than any they would face and time was running out as the spring equinox was fast upon them. They would be needed in the next two or three days, to influence the outcome of the small band of Ninja. But first the lair of the dragon. They stood as the great stone door rolled out to the side of the lair, it was hot, stifling, in fact it did not have a smell, just the heat as they could hear the dragon breath out and suck in oxygen, this wasn't frightful but it wasn't inviting either.

Just as they stepped towards the cavern's mouth the Shaolin Keeper in the Faith of the Dragon spoke, "You do not have to undertake this as the failures of the martial artists that have braved the challenges are nothing but shadow and death".

Shuzi bowed slightly as did the old Shidoshi. They began to enter the cavern. The Shaolin gave another warning and said, "This is your last warning".

They carried on listening and preparing themselves for whatever may come and that would be shadows and death.

*

Romeo and the rest of them drew the symbol to teleport them into Hell. They summoned all the power they could and began the journey into Hell. There was an intense amount of energy as each of them traversed into the fiery pits. They appeared and straight away they were in the thick of the action. Romeo was first to appear and straight away the demons and evil creatures saw Romeo as he appeared. Romeo straight away began to fight throwing razor sharp shuriken at the creatures. Then Jason arrived and he instantly began to use his long chain weapon. Kikeo was next and she began to fight instantly. Then Giros with his katana. And lastly Christian. Who started to pummel and kick into the demons. They were winning as the further forward they got, the more they tried to swarm over them, Romeo decided to use the Summon shadows. It would give them the break they needed to get to Lustran. The spell was powerful and Romeo stood there and made the finger shapes that empowered the spell. And the Demon's that seemed to be swarming over them suddenly ran in fear as the spell did what Romeo hoped for. It showed and clouded the demons and pit fiends with shadows.

Then Romeo marked the place that he had cast the spell so as to know how to get back to the teleportation symbol. He then folded his fingers into the Kanji for strength. This made his strength ten times more powerful. He was getting ahead in the fight, the rest did the same. Demons were running this way and that in fear of the shadows and in fear of the Ninja Romeo. As the further into Hell they got whilst the spell of Shadows was working on their enemies and they made full use of said power.

Christian was particularly lethal and this was as his studies had turned him superhuman, the dragon had truly empowered him. He found his technique had really taken shape, he was thunderously fast and powerfully strong. He was smashing into demons and killing undead without really trying. The shadow spell was working well as it had made all the difference, it still had a short time left but Romeo and the rest of them were going to use this to its full advantage. The spell was doing what it was meant for and that was to scare and terrify the enemies of Romeo, the spell had done a good job and more and more devils, demons and pit fiends had succumbed to the spells power. They were fleeing at the sheer volume of shadows that were spearheading the five Ninja. They were invincible for the mean time. But they knew this wouldn't last as the spell only had a ten-minute duration and they were growing short on time, after that they would be at their mercy. And in the thick of the action. They were killing as many as they could but the spell was growing dimmer. Romeo drew another teleportation sign on the red rock of Hell then they left and went back to the Koga dojos. There would be nine of these short skirmishes. Or until they came upon Lustran. They would need all their skills and powers to be at peak condition. So just as the spell was fading they teleported away. And the shadow's ceased their dangerous dance. The demon howled as it realised it had been tricked and that the army of Ninjas it faced was an illusion. Each demon as it was told by the greater demons howled in tragedy. Lustran realised that he was surrounded by weak and incompetent fools. He made an example of one by biting his head clean of and letting its blood spray up the red rock walls. The hissing of demon as it watched the gruesome lesson sounded out into the molten rock and halls of bone. The entrails of their kills and sacrifices was every-where. They were hoping for another chance at the five Ninja.

*

Meanwhile Shuzi and the old Shidoshi were treading carefully into the resting place of the Golden Dragon. Where it was dead and all its remains had decayed into dust. But still it's spirit lived on and its sacred powers had increased. As each year it decayed, first thing to happen was a steel spike trap that the two of them had to circumnavigate. This was easy for both the boy and the old Shidoshi as they had learned to walk on the air many years ago. It was a pre-requisite of the Ninja. And they managed it easily. They then came to the dragons famous ambush were they saw littered at their feet was a dozen or more bodies. They couldn't see any trap that had been sprung. The old man's keen senses told him that something was very wrong. Then he heard it, it was a small hiss but enough to let the Shidoshi know that they were on the forefront of a major poison. He breathed in through his nostrils and began to slow his pulse down but at the same time step over the bodies. Shuzi did exactly the same, seeing the old Shidoshi make the signal of air. They then carried on further into the lair. The hissing stopped as they got round onto a ledge and further down onto a lip. That led further down into the bowers of the dragon. The old Shidoshi smiled as he looked into the vast dark space that was obviously it's mouth. They traversed further and further avoiding various dart traps and evil acid traps. They did this with a degree of skill. Avoiding to the worst of it then they rested. They ate a small meal of rice balls and some cold acrid green tea that was refreshing and nice on the palate. They then started again to follow the sacred path of the Dragon. This time they knew they were being truly tested as four undead highly animated dead shaolin attacked. No this was not going to be easy. They circled the Shidoshi trying to send them off balance, but Shuzi was quick to react and lopped one of their heads off. The other three Undead Monks went in for the kill but were caught as the old Shidoshi manoeuvred, under its strike and used its own body weight against him. And threw the thing as he ducked under its strike. Then with an empi (elbow) He crushed its ribs. Then sent the undead creature reeling away as it screamed. The Shidoshi after that drew his Katana and began to circle the blade around him keeping the undead monks at bay. Shuzi sailed over the old Shidoshi and came down with a slicing motion halving the creature that was about to strike at the old Shidoshi from the side. That was two that the young Ninja had vanquished and the other two were getting a little unnerved. They both twirled their half knives. The smell was sickening and the two Ninja were beginning to gag slightly. As the two undead decayed rapidly and left a gaseous burst. That was both rank and foul. They again calmed their breathing down and carried on with the task at hand. The other two undead began to circle again. But the Shidoshi and Shuzi closed the distance and stood back-to-back with their katanas aloft. Shuzi measured the distance with his left hand.

He then struck with fury. Bringing the cold tempered steel right down the left side of the undead monk. It was a clean yet an easy strike for Shuzi. Whilst this happened the old Shidoshi with an empty gesture of sizing the things mid-riff. Brought his katana and sliced the thing in two. Again they decayed into gaseous form. The two intrepid Ninja carried on into the heart of the dead dragon. They were nearly there. "A little further" Said the Shidoshi. Shuzi smiled and replied, "Yes Grandad". They then carried on.

*

Meanwhile Romeo and his group of Ninja sat yet again in half lotus. And began again the sacred Kanji shapes and chants. Every once in a while, wisping a sacred shape in the air. Christian had taught them well. After finishing the sets, Jason went back to his studies on demonic death points. It had been a long haul for Jason and he was well battle hardened, and had lots of tricks up his sleeves, and the dim mak points on the demon were just one set of them. He had taken to the task of studying the dragon lore like a duck to water. But then they all did. He was fond of the spells he had learned. In fact, the particular set he had learned was one of the most difficult, and took the most control. It was a spell that created a wall of blood red flame between him and his enemies. This was a good spell as it gave them the opportunity to rejuvenate, but it too had a time limit and could only be used the once. This was still the best plan though. And may give them the opportunity to kill the major demon, Lustran. This was Jason's specialty and he knew that it was a difficult venture. But kept positive knowing how important his part in this was. He would be needed to strike as many deadly blows as he could. This would give Romeo and the rest the opportunity to finish the Tengu Demon.

Chapter 18

Lustran totted up the losses he had endured, and there were many. He had never encountered such losses but knew that he had time left to turn this deadly battle of wits and magic back on the five Ninja. But he felt the cold depths of fear something that he had never felt in at least two decades. But he had survived it then and was sure he could survive it again. He smiled as the smithies were fast in working the dark steel into Katana and various other bladed weapons, like the shuriken. This steel was then imbibed with poison and a lot of mystical curses that helped the dark metal bite and bite deep. He was growing more and more in confidence.

He lifted up a Shizo Katana, which was the size of a tall human. The darkened blade was anointed with hemlock herbs and various other dark poisons. He was curling his lip over his fang and he could taste the ferocity in the air, and could feel the power of the evil Tengu army. They wouldn't be so easily duped the next time. He knelt on his dark and bloody rug and made contact with his Master Sethkis.

"You still failed me Lustran."

Lustran sighed as he heard the hissing voice of his master, "Sorry Master," he replied.

Sethkis snorted in arrogance, "If you fail me again I will dine on your flesh".

Lustran took this to heart and carried on, "We were confused, beguiled and tricked my lord. We will not let it happen again".

Lustran knew that he had better pray that it didn't.

Sethkis hissed again, "You must take care demon, as the old Shidoshi has travelled deep into the Golden Dragons resting place".

Lustran shook his head, "No master I vanquished that old fool."

Sethkis hissed again, "He has just become more powerful demon," Lustran shook his head in disbelief. "He can give no assistance Master, I am sure of it".

Sethkis waited a moment and let his thoughts settle. "You be sure demon that he doesn't gain an advantage, or the very pits and bowers of hell may suffer" Lustran again sighed and replied, "I will do what I can" Sethkis grew angry at this statement and replied, "You will do it if you fail me again, as I said I will feast on your flesh". He then hissed and vanished out of the bone and blood chamber. Lustran sneered at himself and decided to make an example of two of his hardest and best demons, demons who had shown courage and great malice in many battles. Yes, they had seen to the demon Coltar, but knew that the fight had only begun. Lustran beheaded one of his best and malicious Tengu. Nobody had seen this coming. The second was a lesser devil who had stayed in the fray right up until the Ninja left. Lustran ripped the devils horned head off, as he gripped his horns, he then, with Supernatural strength tore him in two. Leaving the entrails and organs strewn across the chamber, its dark viscose blood pumped slowly out of the severed remains of the devil. Lustran laughed as the rest of the Tengu Demons gulped dry hot air.

They were two of the best that Lustran had destroyed and everybody knew it. They would rather fall on their Katanas than suffer the wrath of Lustran. But until they ended up masterless they had a hell of a fight in front of them and it was Lustran's deadly pleasure of killing that stood out, not torture, not maiming, but the delight he took in drinking blood of an inferior and feasting on the flesh, if not just Humans, but demons too. He went back to his antechamber and began to sharpen his Katana. He took great pleasure in making examples of certain Demons and devils.

*

Shuzi and the Shidoshi wandered through to the rear room where the dragon had melted gold, silver, platinum and copper. Also the floor was encrusted with sapphires, diamonds, pearls and rubies, these had been subject to intense dragons fire. And had melted into the precious metals. Shuzi looked at the cache with his mouth open. The treasure was luring him, drawing him to try and steal some of it. But it was obvious that it lay waiting in the form of a subtle trap. The old Shidoshi grabbed Shuzi by the sleeve and said, "It's a trap".

Shuzi heeded his warning and walked over the treasure. The Shidoshi spotted the workings of the trap, a glass bowl holding a large vat of acid that would pour over their heads soon as they so much as laid a finger on the treasure. it hadn't been sprung which meant that no one had made it this far. They carried on to the belly of the wyrm. Where they experienced a great uneasiness. A fear that made their hair stand on end. The Shidoshi was ready for anything so was the young boy, Shuzi.

They carried into the deep chasm of the innards of the warm. Coming across more dart traps and more treasure traps. They did the right thing and avoided both. Only springing the traps after they had got past them. This was to insure a safe passage back. They eventually made it past the Belly and could hear the wind move and whistle along the innards of the dragon. It was surprising to the two of them they had circumnavigated the entire beast and hadn't even taken a scratch. They got to the tail that tapered off into the rock. There before them they saw a chest with a complicated dragon lock. Shuzi smiled and began to pick the lock of the chest.

*

Romeo and the rest of the Ninjas had rested well. And the witching hour was coming upon them, but still the spring equinox was on their side. They had a week until the longest day then they would strike a final blow and probably shut down Hell. Seal it shut with a Japanese Shinto priest blessing the way. Making sure that the teleportation marking was null and void for demon and evil doer. They set up another Kanji symbol, enabling the group of Ninja to pass into the circles of Hell. The closer to pandemonium (the circle of devils that control all of Hell), the closer they would be to death. They had a lot to contend with. But knew in their hearts that they would be successful. They had a distinct advantage and that was the Ancient Golden Dragon scrolls. They had learned most of it, the rest lay hidden in the dragons tomb. That was exactly what they thought, the old Shidoshi would be doing. He would come through even though they were dead and in the spirit world.

Romeo rested his mind's eye on the old Shidoshi and Shuzi who was busy picking the grand master lock on the chest of the dragon. He slipped the skeleton key next to serrated tool and, "Their," He said as the lock opened and the iron and golden lock fell to the ground.

They opened the chest and low and behold, the last three scrolls of dragon's fire. The ancient martial arts text that showed how to walk on flame and various other ways to trick the enemy with its own weapons and its own minds. The flames that seemed to be around them suddenly grew still and it was like the dragon breathed a huge sigh on the other side. Then all the traps that they hadn't encountered sprung and there were a few that by luck and guile they had not triggered. The way was clear to them. It gave them a sense of purpose, a way in, which they could help the Ninja group in its struggle against the Tengu Army of Demons.

Romeo smiled as one of the Jian circled the two and showed the symbol that the Old Shidoshi needed to draw in order for the scrolls to land in the Ninja Christian's hands. He smiled as a light shone through one of his windows and the light was that of the spring new moon. The scrolls appeared and Christian bowed to the moon and saw the light land and the scrolls, the last of the dragon scrolls, materialized on the table.

Christian smiled knowing that all the pit fiends in Hell were no match for Golden Dragons fire. Romeo knocked, gently on the study door and waited to be asked to enter. Christian did so. Romeo bowed as Christian held aloft in his hands the ancient dragons scroll of fire. Romeo was immersed in its hallow glow and its presence showed as all the lights led back into it. And it irradiated so, so much so, that he had to cover his eyes and all that its glow touched was bathed in gold. He smiled and rested his eye's in the radiant glow bathing in its awe, a holy baptism indeed, that was the thought that went through his mind. They would truly have the power to destroy the demon Lustran.

*

Christian started immediately to read and acknowledge it's true power. It was an immortal blessing and one that they couldn't help but be grateful for, all the scrolls that they had and all the power that they summoned. It was a gift from the gods and deities and they knew it. The dragon had lain his life down in protection for the world and his subordinates and pupils had written the scrolls, sealing them in dragons blood. Then as the dragon lay down and died a great calm and peace radiated around the world. And all the world knew that the last of the great golden ones had passed away and left in serenity and in the wisdom of peace, it had shown great gratitude to its pupils and subordinates.

They each, a total of ten, began the journey into the heart of China, where they would study and train a select few. Shaolin Kung Fu was born. That in turn led to Japan paying homage to the dragon then the rest of Asia. The scrolls and the remains of the dragon vanished into the Jin-Go world. The masters only had a small part of the wisdom of the Golden Dragon. The rest lay dormant in the Jin-Go world and was watched over by the greatest of monks and martial artists. The ones who successfully traversed into that realm and were courageous enough to try and attain the dragons wisdom. None had survived the passage into the dragon's entrance. And few had lived to even try and tame the dragons fire.

Chapter 19

Romeo and the rest of his group were busy polishing off their martial arts studies when Christian gave off a great big ecstatic scream (Like he had just won the Lottery) Giros shook his head and muttered in Japanese, "Clown". Then carried on studying his Kuji Kirri. He was learning how to grow in power with his body mass and everything growing. Also his strength, which he would need tripled and his muscles flexed and he could pull of a series of feats such as the bending of bars and the lifting of incredible weight. He was also a master of digging into hot rocks with his hands and it was the large size of rock's which he was turning into dust. Kikieo was practicing her flying kick techniques. This was becoming like second nature to her, she too was practicing Kuji Kirri and Ketsu. She had grown in power with the sacred words and shapes and was an adept at both healing and Psionics. The gift of the last scroll of the Golden Dragon had opened up the doorway into more paths and more lessons, more divinity more power. He was in his element, speaking in dragons tongue. A language that had died out thousands of years ago. He smiled and clicked out a syllable in the dragons tongue. Then placed his fingers into a Kanji shape and waited. The wait was quite some time as the symbols began to form a small picture and this was one, the dragon egg.

"Hah!" he shouted then walked into the hallway, smiling in pride as the things he had learned were just the beginning. No he was learning how to reincarnate and also how to find an ancient place where the dragon had laid an egg. And that egg had been fertilised by the dragons lover, so he was a she all along. He smiled at the other four and said, "She has laid an egg".

Romeo saw that Christian was excited, so he ceased what he was practicing. "Okay Christian San," he said. "Where?"

Christian smiled recognising Romeos mood and it was genuine surprise. "Well its somewhere in Tibet" Romeo smiled and said, "Yes Christian, but where?"

*

Lustran continued to meditate on the task at hand. That was the fact that the last of the dragons scrolls had been found and that they would make Romeo and his band of Ninja's double in strength. Lustran was still optimistic as he too had magic. It was the darkest of magic. Born of blood and suffering. The heart of a virgin child. The mind of a pure scholar, Lustran's powers were of the darkest magic. He only kept the most diabolical of company. Always ate flesh. And was never consumed with compassion or love, no, these things were alien to him. He had given up all thoughts of goodness when he had first twisted into the evil shape that was now him. He had no recourse to the Lord or Buddha. No he was diabolical, evil, malevolent. He had become the evil sinister shape of terror. Most of the other demons stayed on his good side. Those that walked in his shadow and tainted the thoughts of Lustran usually found themselves on his dinner plate, he had no time for weakness. And that reflected in his mood and habits. He didn't hesitate or think twice about killing and eating a subordinate. He dined fresh and dined regularly. His evil hunger only slightly appeased at the various times that he killed, ate and partook of the blood of a lower caste demon. He was revered and respected, also worshipped as one of the evilest and dangerous of demons. He carried on meditating and then stood up and began to go through the demon tengu Katas. He finished the kata with a sharp hiss as he moulded the Kia points expertly into the foundations of the Kata. Knowing each point was a vital point, on the enemies' body. And he was an adept at fighting two or three opponents at the same time. This was why the strength of the Kata was in the Kia points. He did the Kata and didn't even break sweat.

*

Romeo was in the middle of a deep concentration exercise. He had done well in the studies of the dragon, but still he was no expert. He caught fire in the way of the dragon. And began the balancing and stance of the dragon, 'For something that had died a thousand years ago we still know its way'. he thought as he went through the dragon set. He was sending thunderous half inch punches. And deadly dragon kicks. He also shifted into dragon claws. A skill that took years to master and was pinpoint accurate. He had only been learning the style a few days. But had landed on the right side of the dragon. He was already on his way to becoming a master. And this discipline was an unusual one. As the dragon had repeatedly shown its difficulties in the training and usage of the style. But Romeo kept up the discipline. Knowing that it was more than just a combat style it was an artform. It showed beauty and wonder. And a yearning for more, more, more. It was something that Romeo based on its subtle beauty and high-octane destructive powers.

There was much to be learned. And Romeo was thirsty for the knowledge. He carried on the dragon set. Memorizing each of the subtle points that were Dim Mak. And not to be treated lightly. He had plenty of training to help him through the set. It was not dissimilar to Tiger. Yet at the same time more powerful. He was making progress. So were the rest of them. They were doing the studies of dragon magic. The deep arcane sorcery that had made the dragon the most fearsome of enemies. Its spells sent the enemies into panic, And it didn't matter how evil and sinister they were. They still wouldn't have the strength to destroy the powers of the dragon. They fell into a deep meditative state that was constantly vigilant yet constantly at peace. This was a strength in itself. To be that calm, yet ready for anything. To be on a higher level of thought. To be swimming in mysticism. The power words, the interlocking of fingers the shapes that they made as they got further and further into nirvana.

Christian was showing each one a different path. Yet each lesson had subtlety and much to learn. They were never short of experience in the ways of the dragon. Christian had seen to that. He carried on making the dragon noises that was the tongue of the dragon. He hissed and clicked and rasped through his throat. Each word making sense and thought from very little information. He was like a kid in a candy store. He carried on smiling as he uncovered new secrets, new ways. Knowing only that the power in those scrolls may be the only weapon that they had to combat the darkness of the Tengu Demons. This remained a fact that the only strength they had was written in the blood of dragons. And well it remained a cold hard fact they would need all their skills to fight. They carried on in the meditations and invoked the very spirit of the dragon. It was a power that was both subtle and grand.

*

Shuzi smiled as they completed, their meditations and went to the Golden Dragons hall to pay homage to the dragon. It had taken many years and many martial artists had tried to tame the savagery of the dragon. Few even ventured into its lair as it gave of a distinct feeling of both power and fear. They took great joy from having accomplished the journey and succeeding where many had failed to even get to. The old Shidoshi began to prepare, his spirit and soul to help the band of Ninjas. In what was their greatest of challenges, the Tengu demons and specifically, Lustran. The Old Shidoshi smiled as he settled into a way, a challenge, that had been very difficult yet rewarding at the same time. Shuzi smiled and began to do his Kata, he was really empowered by the whole dragon and it had changed his senses. Making them more powerful more in tune with the Universe. He was at the peak of his abilities and that made him both dangerous and revered. The spirit that he had was running through his body, turning everything to gold, he took on a shimmer. A glow that was all around him. He could see great distances especially in his mind's eye. Whereas the Shidoshi was learning a very different kind of way. A way in which to use his mind as a weapon, also a way to shield his body from multiple attacks. This was all part of the way of the Dragon. They carried on with little sleep but at the same time they felt invigorated as if the act of the martial art in itself was as easy as breathing. The grandad and his grandson, had made the power of the dragon a part of them. They could do things that no one else could do and see things no one else could see. They were preparing themselves to help out Romeo and the rest of the Ninja. They would be at full strength in a couple of days.

Chapter 20

Meanwhile Romeo and his band of Ninja were gaining more and more power. The scrolls were showing them techniques and magic that had been lost for centuries, they were beginning to become immortals. You know ghosts that walk, They had no fear, and this was well, this was a true gift of the gods. The dragon had reincarnated and given its soul to the Ninja. Romeo crackled with lightning as he went through the elements of true power. He made the shape of air then caused a small amount of friction that sent lightning snaking across the room and striking the Chong at the back of the room and splitting it in two. He then carried on wrapping lightning about his body sending the occasional bolt of lightning snaking at various targets. Destroying them he laughed as he done so, knowing now how lethal he was. He shaped the bright white bolts of electricity, becoming more and more adept at the skill of folding lightning. The rest of them smiled as they watched Romeo grow in power. Kikieo was still studying the Psionics and mastering the use and strength of her mind. She too had become an adept at the dragons spirit. She was lifting things heavy weights with her mind. And sending off a piercing scream that split the ear drums of everyone. Jason was doing his Kata and sending off a shimmer that eventually turned into a mirror image of himself. Giros was bending bars with his bare hands. Practically tying the bar into a knot. Christian was practicing a flaming fist, a technique that had been lost for thousands of years. It sent a huge ball of fire that engulfed the enemy incinerating them. They began to prepare them-selves for the next attack of the Demons.

*

Lustran gathered his generals and prepared to launch a very definite and decisive attack. It would either make or break them. The underling's he wasn't caring about, but the generals, the lesser demons, well he knew they would be needed. As they were very competent in the skills of martial arts and its spiritual prowess. They were indeed a powerful enemy and they too had spells and powers.

Lustran smiled as the demons began to gather, he then began to speak, "My worthy friends, my unholy weapons against nature. You are my disciples, my right hand against god. We will finish this that started thousands of years ago. We must claim the Earth realms. We mustn't fail our hierarchy. We must celebrate in the wake of the dead benevolent force that has stood before us for all this time"

He stood and raised his arms there was a great uproar at the base of the cliff where he stood. "We must succeed, we must punish all things holy".

There was another uproar. Then Lustran came down the mountain pillar of Pandemonium and started to head into the Earth Realms. He was carrying a huge Shizo Katana. One which he could and would wield deftly. They would attack at the end of the day knowing the night was all the power they needed.

*

Romeo smiled as he began to stretch the lightning charm that he had imbibed. He was still fully in charge of the ability and knew it would not let him down. Kikieo stood in the field where the Gate to Hell was and readied herself. This wasn't going to be easy. And she knew it would take every ounce of skill and power to succeed in this monstrous task. The rest of the group joined her and, Romeo was truly at peace in this time, he had surpassed all the expectations and become at one with the nature of lightning. Christian smiled and became on with fire. And Giros he was one with Metal, They weren't going out easy that was for sure. Romeo produced his two Kama and wore yet again the Tiger Gi of the Koga.

They rested and started to channel through their spirits. Each one of them becoming more and more at ease with the spirit of the dragon. Their energies crackled with the spirit of the dragon they had nothing to lose, yet everything to prove. They knew they were the only ones who could defeat Lustran and the Hordes of Hell that had just appeared on the field. First there was a great mist then they could hear their footsteps as they walked on the common. Romeo wrapped electricity around his hands and the Kama he held then fired of a series of chain strikes against the front ranks that were running at them. Kikieo was lifting and bashing their skulls in, using telekinetic powers that she had become attuned with. Christian unleashed a mass of fireballs at them.

Jason on the other hand was waiting for the melee to come closer. He would then use his powers to confuse and beguile them. Then he would be able to fight them tooth and nail. Giros was ripping up huge rocks, twice his size and throwing them at the mass of demons. This went on for a good fifteen minutes. With Romeo and his friends doing immense damage. Then the skies opened and it began to rain. This put a dampener on the spirits of the Tengu Deamons. Who thought the weather would be a hindrance to Romeo but no this only encouraged the Ninja to fight fiercer. They settled their skills down and decided to do the rest hand-to-hand.

Lustran was at the rear and making a huge partition in the ranks of his demons. He walked forth and faced the very challenge of Romeo and his friends. That was when Jason struck and struck hard. He aimed his shuken at the neck of Lustran, to one of the points that would do most damage. It hit but was not enough to stop the colossal demon. So he aimed the next two, one at its midriff the other at his side, Then Romeo stepped forward and began to fold lightning and sent a bolt to each of the shuken Jason had thrown. He began to scream as the lightning coursed through his body, this caused a significant amount of damage. Slowing the said demon down. Then he took a swipe at Jason who was back flipping away. Dodging his massive Katana. Giros saw the two of them in a fierce pitch battle so he decided to help. He picked up another boulder and sent it hurling at Lustran. That put Lustran off his pace. Giving Romeo yet another chance at sending forth lightning. And again it caused the monstrous demon to scream out in pain.

He then held himself together and flung a deadly shuriken of his own at Jason. Who crumpled as the thing bit deep into his left breast, skewering his heart. Romeo watched as the demon finished off Jason. Christian also saw as the monstrous demon smashed the Ninjas head with the butt of his sword. Killing Jason. Romeo and Christian, both at the same time began to weave their abilities into a catastrophic chain of fire and lightning. They nearly finished the unholy thing. But they were suddenly overcome by numbers of Tengu Demon, despite Kikieo doing her best to keep them at bay. Giros on the other hand was killing them with great ease. His strength growing, like an energy dynamo, he kept getting stronger and stronger as he got more and more into the fray.

The four of them were truly in trouble, they knew that this was the end for them. They were being swarmed over and had little hope of winning this deadly dance. But Giros was ripping and striking at the demons as they encroached upon him. Romeo was standing free with the lightning crackling out him. He began to target the leaders of the hordes of hell. They were sending them forth into the paths of the Ninja. Christian was summoning the powers of fire and was incinerating them three four at a time. Kikieo was lifting and bashing the brains of two or three demons at a time.

Kikieo was awash with psychic energy and doing things to the enemy that no mortal person should see or even hear of. Romeo was still dealing with Lustran and he wasn't going down without a fight. The all-consuming force of Tengu Demons was getting a taste of benevolent dragons powers. Jason had fallen but not in vain, the last of the demons spilled out the fiery chasm and started to join the fray where they were gaining more and more strength in their own right in their own strength. The end was near and Lustran had adapted to the power of the lightning. And Romeo was losing momentum, losing the power of the lightning. Christian too was losing his abilities, and more and more demons were coming into the battle.

They were still at an advantage and that advantage was soon shown when the Spirit of the old Shidoshi entered as a true force of the dragon. Shuzi to, was coming into the fight. The old Shidoshi turned into the shape of the dragon and began to devour and, bone crunch after bone crunch, began to devour the enemy. He was working with cataclysmic effect. The innards and all its parts were devoured and digested by the dragon. Shuzi on the other hand was riding said dragon. And being a-good-guide, he helped the best he could. With the spirit and strength of the dragon they began to turn the fight round in their favour. Again the demons began to lose morale. And their cowardice took over and they began to run away from the Ninja's.

Lustran was not going out that easy. He began to murmur and chant summoning a huge cone of power that he sent straight at the dragon. Romeo kept up his attack with the lightning and Christian carried on sending fireballs at Lustran. The flames engulfed the demon just as he finished and sent his cone at the dragon. The dragon crashed onto the ground, down but not out. Romeo sent a huge chain of lightning the most powerful one yet, at the huge demon. And Christian sent a massive, huge ball of fire at him. The dragon picked himself up and walked towards the demon readying himself to devour the demon.

The Demon was engulfed by both lightning and fire. A deadly and accurate combination. He tried to summon one more spell and that was a portal back to the realms of hell. He got to the final chant and began to scream in pain at the powers of the two Ninja. Then crunch as the teeth of the Dragon bit into him and caused the demon more pain that he had ever known. No, there was no sanctuary for the demon but then he had brought it onto himself. The rest of the demons were either obliterated or were hiding like cowards in the underworld of hell. They finished the battle and went and buried Jason Kendricks in the holy ground at the rear of the Koga Dojo's. Shuzi and the old Shidoshi went back into the Jin Go spirit world as did Romeo. Their job being done and done well.

The End